The Thief 's Son

CHRIS SANDERS

A CIP catalogue record for this title is available from the
British Library

First published by Black Coppice Books 2014

The Thief's Son
By
Chris Sanders

www.chrissanderswriter.com

ISBN-10: 1499646569

ISBN-13: 979-1499646566

To

Allen, Dad, Kim and Mum

for all your love and support

TABLE OF CONTENTS

1

An Englishman Abroad

His journey from Caquetá had taken two days longer than planned. The reason for the delay was common in Colombia, especially down south. A bus jammed full with foreign backpackers had been stopped by rebels whilst travelling between cities. The lucky travellers were those who'd been taken hostage. The others, too many to march through thick jungle in one go, had been shot. The usual story.

Samuel stood in the middle of the road, his camera and backpack slung over his shoulder. He'd bought the camera ten years ago for his first assignment back in Sarajevo and the atrocities he'd witnessed in Yugoslavia had stuck with him ever since. Now having spent two months in Colombia, covering its rebel uprising, he had a whole new set of painful memories added to his collection.

As he walked towards the nearest kerb, a large group of Colombian peasants bustled past him. He let them scuttle past, each of them dirty, grubby looking farmers who were returning from a hard day's work on what little land they owned a few miles from town. Watching them disappear amidst the twisting alleyways up ahead, it occurred to Samuel how different in appearance he was compared with most Colombians: Taller than average, fair skinned and with thinning, light brown hair he would never blend in. A sitting target? Perhaps. An ominous thought.

Behind Samuel the bus began to pull away, a cloud of thick smoke momentarily engulfing him. Stepping slowly from the roadside, he started to follow the string of small, whitewashed buildings which made up the town's main high street.

Doncella was like any other slum town in Colombia. Potholes filled with filthy rainwater lined the roads in either direction. Women used them to wash their clothes in. Street kids used them to play in.

"Hey, Americano! You gotta light for me Americano?"

Samuel stopped, glancing down to his left. A skinny black kid wearing a torn grey T-shirt sat with his back against a cafe wall, holding out a crooked cigarette. He was twelve, maybe thirteen and so old enough to carry a gun and fight a rebel war like a lot of other kids in Colombia were being forced to do.

"Hey, you hear what I say?" the boy repeated, waving the cigarette for effect.

"I'm English."

"Whatever, you gotta light?"

Samuel pulled a silver lighter from his trouser pocket and dropped to one knee. He had to be careful. If the other kids spotted him he knew he'd be surrounded in seconds, and he didn't have enough cash to simply give away.

"There you go," Samuel spoke, igniting the ash.

The boy whipped out a small brush from beneath his shirt and began to scrub Samuel's muddied boots. Samuel smiled at the boy's initiative, and climbed back to his feet.

"Now you give me Plata English, you see I got your boots real nice and clean," the boy then lied.

"Soy trabajadara Si?"

"I don't speak Spanish kid, but nice try anyhow," Samuel replied, trying to sound as cool as possible. It didn't work. As soon as he turned his back the boy sprang to his feet, pulling out a long, rusted blade which he'd hidden down the back of his pants.

"Now you give me plata!" he repeated.

Lo Colombia. That's what the locals called it. Mad Colombia. Samuel had been in the country only a couple of months and already he'd witnessed first-hand how crazy a place could get if it let itself. To the far south of Colombia the rebels were stepping up their armed campaign against the government. Across the region, town mayors were being ordered to leave or face execution. Locals who were thought to be in support of the government were being tortured, raped and killed. Hell, it was a free for all. For eight weeks Samuel had been risking his neck traveling from one small town to the next, witnessing the rebels and their brutality at work.

He'd taken photos. Good photos, the sort of shots picture galleries would pay a fortune for if he could get out of Colombia alive. Doncella would be his last town. The last stop and then back to Blighty, back to London and some sort of normality. His luck was running out. He'd had too many close calls over the last eight weeks and now it was time to quit, head on home.

"Give me plata quick English or I slit your throat!" the boy continued, growing more agitated by the second, pressing the point of the blade hard into Samuel's chin. Already it had caused bleeding.

"You hear what I say English?"

Carefully, Samuel reached into his shirt top pocket and, between thumb and forefinger, retrieved a crisp twenty dollar note.

"Here, that's all I got."

With his free hand the boy quickly stuffed the note into his pocket and took a step back.

"I want more English."

"I don't have any more."

"Camera, you give me the camera," he went on, sticking the knife back into Samuel's blooded chin.

"Then you go?" Samuel mumbled.

"Si, then I go," the boy replied, wondering what else he could thieve once he had the camera. The backpack?

Slowly, Samuel began to remove the camera's thick, leather strap from his shoulder. The boy couldn't stop grinning.

"I guess your mother doesn't make enough dollars for you both?" Samuel spoke once the strap was tight in his hand.

"Que?" the boy replied, not really listening, his attention fixed on the camera.

"When she's out begging on the street...She makes you enough?"

The boy's eyes shot up. A moment of hesitation, confusion followed. Had the crazy English guy just said that?

As the boy's lips began to curl in anger, Samuel seized the moment and cracked the solid weight of the camera hard across the skull. Immediately the blade fell to the dust, the boy crumpling a couple of seconds later.

"Like I said, that's all I had to give," Samuel continued, bending over the unconscious kid and snatching back his twenty dollar note.

Now it was sure time to leave. A group of curious locals were already gathering some way down the street, conversing with one another and gesticulating in his general direction. Picking the nearest alleyway, he left the boy and set off at a steady jog through a collection of rubbish strewn isles until the street and its growing mob were out of sight. Lo Colombia. Mad Colombia. Always carry a decoy bundle of cash when travelling through rough parts of town. Play it cool and if you're lucky the bad guys will leave you alone. Ten dollars to a kid from slum city is a lot of money. Of course there were other rules to follow too. Other rules that he'd occasionally broken.

Walking through the barrios with an expensive camera slung about your neck was just inviting trouble, especially late at night. But without a camera close at hand you couldn't shoot film, and you never knew when that next great shot was going to pop up. So, during the whole two months in Colombia, Samuel had always kept the camera at the ready. Another calculated risk. Another sure sign he was pushing his luck.

The alley opened out. Breathless, he fell against its nearest wall, knocking over a bucket full of rubbish and sending a score of huge, dirty rats scurrying for cover. A hotel stood opposite. A group of young girls milled around its open doorway, waving and smiling at him. It was getting late and he was tired. Back down the alley, when he listened very carefully, he could hear a mix of angry voices growing louder.

The hotel/brothel opposite seemed like the only safe option. The rooms wouldn't be much, but then the hostels around this part of town would only offer him the same standard of comfort and at a slightly higher price.

"Welcome to hotel Yuldonna! Americano?" the short, balding man in his early forties spoke. A thin, black moustache lived beneath his long, narrow nose and as he spoke his fingers gently toyed with it.

"No, I'm English."

"English! Well, what would you like to drink?"

"I'll just take the room if that's okay?"

"Then what about a girl? We got lots of pretty girls; you have any one you want."

Samuel let his backpack lean against the counter and glanced quickly towards the small group of poor girls who sat huddled in the far corner of the bar looking bored, then back to the brothel's owner, who still toyed with his moustache.

"I'll just take the room. One room, one night, understood?"

The owner shrugged and turned slowly to face the full rack of keys which hung directly behind him.

"There you go, room six," he continued, slapping the key down onto the wooden counter with a look of rejection across his fat face. Not bothering to reply, Samuel slipped the key into his shirt pocket.

"You pay a week in advance, okay?"

"I'm only here for one night," Samuel replied.

The owner rolled his eyes, having heard it all before.

"Then it will be ten dollars."

Samuel paid the man.

"You go up the stairs and it's the third on the right," the owner continued, no longer playing with his moustache. Samuel picked up his backpack and headed towards the long flight of stairs adjacent to the counter.

~ ~ ~

Room number six was just like any other cheap room he'd found whilst staying in small town Colombia. Nothing special. Apart from the bed and washbasin, only a towel; a tiny piece of used soap and a roll of toilet paper existed. The toilet, Samuel knew, would be hidden somewhere down a dimly lit corridor that he had no intention of locating until it became imperative to do so.

He fell against the hard mattress, letting his arm drape across his face, but woke when he heard the telephone ringing, only deciding to find the machine when its ring became unrelenting.

"Yes..Who is this?"

"You pay for phone calls too English, okay?" the owner barked down the line.

"Fine," Samuel replied, replacing the receiver and stuffing the ancient contraption back under the bed where he'd found it. He'd been asleep for perhaps an hour, when, upon waking he'd found his cramped quarters filled with dark shadows. As he struggled out of bed, threw open the wooden shutters, a long, narrow street with no sunlight faced him.

Halfway down this street, as he looked to the right, he spotted a second hotel. Only this one seemed to be doing a lot more business. A wild succession of flashing lights blazed out from each of its windows and deep inside loud Vallenato folk music and frenzied conversation spilled onto the street. A fiesta was brewing. The Colombians loved their parties. Even with their country in such a terrible state they still knew how to enjoy themselves, a testament to their national character.

Further down the street a large crowd of people had gathered, and were now making their way towards the two hotels, each of them boasting a silleta full of flowers on their back. Hard though he tried Samuel couldn't remember the name of this particular festival, but he remembered seeing larger versions while staying in bigger cities like Medellin to the north. Soon fireworks would be lit, there would be more music, more noise. Samuel checked his watch. It would be early morning back in London, and sooner or later he'd have to find the courage and phone his editor, who'd been expecting him back for over a week now. He sat back on the bed, dragged the phone from its hiding place, and began to tap in the numbers.

"Yeah?" a gruff voice – his editor's voice – answered after almost thirty, very long seconds.

"John..."

"Who's this?"

Samuel hesitated. He could still hang up, think up a list of watertight excuses and perhaps save himself a shed load of grief.

"Who the hell is this?" the gruff voice continued down the line.

Samuel knew he should have waited until lunch was over. His boss had usually downed a few pints by then, and generally behaved like a rational human being for the rest of the day,

"It's Samuel...Samuel Locke."

A pause. The line crackled.

"I said it's Samuel...Samuel Locke," he repeated.

"Not the young man we sent to Colombia? The little creep who was due back over two weeks ago?"

"I'm afraid so, John."

"So where the hell are you? Have the rebels stopped their fighting?"

"I have your shots, John."

"Oh, you have my photographs hey?"

"Decent shots too, you're going to love them, I promise."

"Well do I get to see them sometime soon Samuel? We don't want to rush you or anything but you've already missed the last two deadlines!"

Leaving the bed, Samuel leant against the window frame, phone caught between shoulder and chin as he sparked up a cigarette, watching as the parade below began to pass by the second hotel.

"I'll be back first thing Monday, John."

"First thing Monday? It's Tuesday today Sammy boy!"

"I know, but there's not a whole lot I can do about the situation."

That was a lie. There was a whole lot he could do. He estimated a crowd of maybe a hundred people gathering below his window. He could sink a few beers himself. Chase a few girls. Hell, this was Colombia. Lo Colombia. He could do anything he wanted.

"You still there Samuel?"

"Yeah, I'm still here John," Samuel replied, taking a long, slow drag on his dying cigarette.

"Your job's on the line Sammy. Don't care how good you think you are. We run a team effort here. No room for loners. You understand?"

"I understand."

~ ~ ~

They could stick the job. He was good enough to earn a tidy sum working freelance. He took risks. He liked to take risks. The picture libraries loved him. One day, damn it, he'd own his very own picture library. He was still young. He could still make it big. He was still in control of his own destiny. To hell with the lousy magazine.

"You out of money yet?"

"I still got enough to get back."

"Good, because we can't afford to finance your lavish life style any more. You got that Samuel?"

"Every word John, every word."

Samuel was still looking out the window as he'd replied, only now his eyes were sharp, searching. He'd seen something, someone out of place. More than that. He'd recognized a face, a face from his distant past. His unhappy past.

"Sammy? You still there?"

"Yeah, yeah, I'm still here."

"Now don't you go ignoring me! Don't you even dare!"

Samuel wasn't listening. His eyes were stuck on the passing parade. He'd caught a glimpse of a figure, a lean figure mingling in amongst the growing mob down below. A figure that stood painfully out of place in comparison to those who surrounded him, pushed into him: A very tall old man who wore a loose, white cotton suit.

"Samuel! Answer me damn it!" the voice at the end of the line continued to rave. Again, Samuel ignored it, waiting for the crowd to part, to reveal its hidden visitor for a second time.

The crowd did part. Samuel let his cigarette slip from his mouth and fall to the room's grubby tiles, his keen eyes still following the old man as he'd quickly ducked through the packed doorway of the second hotel.

"Dad..." he then whispered, his face pressed up against the window.

"Sammy, Sammy! I know you can hear me, what the hell are you playing at?"

"I have to go now John...See you Tuesday."

"Don't hang up on me Samuel, and it's Monday damn it! You come back Monday!" Slowly, Samuel replaced the receiver.

~ ~ ~

"Ola Senor...You like T-shirt? Nice T-shirt."

Samuel brushed the kid to one side, reaching the doorway to the second hotel only a few seconds before a new set of street urchins spotted him and pounced.

"Ten dollars friend," the large gorilla on the door spoke, the palm of his huge, dirty hand pressing into Samuel's chest just as soon as he'd arrived at the hotel.

Knowing he was being ripped off, Samuel dug out a ten dollar note and peered into the hotel's bustling lobby. There was no sign of his father. He could see large groups of Colombians singing and dancing; but the only Europeans present at that moment appeared to be a handful of young backpackers who stood looking self-conscious beside the bar. Once the toll had been paid, the gorilla raised his arm. Samuel pushed by and soon found himself squeezing through the merry band of partygoers before reaching the bar proper.

"Se sube a pie y se baja en ambulancia!" a short, elderly man with rotting teeth and a great deal of grey hair began to whisper into Samuel's ear.

The Colombian was quite drunk, and as he leant his frail body towards Samuel, significant amounts of beer in his unsteady glass began to slop over the rim. Samuel stepped back.

"Careful there chief," he had to warn, hoping the drunk would take the hint and quietly sidle off.

"Que?"

"Domingas! Isientate!"

From behind the bar a stout, middle-aged woman leaned over and gave the unruly drunk a sharp clip about his ear. Looking somewhat confused, the elderly man shuffled away, staggering towards the group of backpackers, hoping for a better audience. The youngsters nervously watched his approach.

"Don't worry about old Domingas, what can I get you?" the barmaid then spoke, gently brushing back her dark fringe which had fallen loose from its tight bun. She was no older than fifty, quite stocky in build and managed to keep her light green eyes firmly on Samuel throughout their ensuing conversation.

"I'm looking for a guy, a European wearing a white suit. He's tall, has silver hair. He came in here not long before me. He calls himself Jack Locke, you seen him?"

The barmaid suddenly flushed as she heard the name mentioned and seemed to struggle to find her next words.

"You're looking for a guy? What about a young girl? We have plenty of young girls," she nervously replied.

Samuel leant forward.

"Listen, the man I'm looking for is my father!"

"Your Papa? You go and lose your own Papa?"

"Can you just tell me where he went? It's very important."

Again the barmaid hesitated, this time her eyes glanced off towards somebody seated behind Samuel.

"No, I see nobody like that come in here...You go try some other bar maybe."

"He was in here not five minutes ago, you must have seen him!"

"I told you, nobody like that in here. Now you buy drink or go."

Samuel began to scan the lobby. Apart from the backpackers the only other Westerner to spark any interest sat directly behind him, playing cards with some of the locals.

The chap looked around sixty, his hair grey and untidy. Short and plump in body, he wore a crumpled, short sleeved white shirt and a pair of white trousers, both of which had seen better days. A large mound of cigarette butts, one or two still smoking, sat next to his stack of cards; and every few seconds he took a steady sip from a pint of Columbiana. Occasionally his eyes would squint from the surrounding smoke, his lightly tanned skin badly creased from years of such squinting. Still, the man wasn't his father.

"You want a drink or not?" the barmaid continued, having noticed Samuel's new interest and growing quite annoyed.

"Do you have a toilet here?" Samuel replied quickly.

"Que?"

"Toilet! Where are your toilets?"

Giving Samuel a strange look, the barmaid pointed towards a battered door a few paces from the bar.

"Then you buy drink!" she snapped, but Samuel was long gone.

The toilet cubicles were empty except for one. Samuel stood against the far wall, opposite the locked cubicle. If the other people who entered noticed him waiting, they only bothered to give him a brief glance, all too eager to re-join the festivities outside. Slowly, the cubicle door began to open. Samuel straightened himself, still not sure what his first move would be if indeed it was his estranged father who stumbled out. Hit him? Talk to him? He'd play it by ear. At least give the chap a chance to explain before laying into him. Only polite. He thought of his poor mother as the door gradually opened and felt a sudden, but pleasant rush of testosterone course through his veins.

Automatically, his right fist clenched. He took a couple of steps forward, and as the overweight

Colombian appeared, still struggling to buckle up his belt, he very nearly threw a punch. Instead, he could only freeze and watch as the bemused local hurriedly left. Leaving the toilets himself, Samuel wandered back into the bar. Stepping quietly through the revellers he found the card-playing Westerner now chatting to the barmaid.

"You find your Papa?" she spoke with a smile as Samuel appeared. As he did, the Westerner left the bar and reseated himself. Samuel shook his head.

"Maybe you didn't see him after all?"

"It was him."

Taking a glass from beneath the bar, she began to pour him a drink.

"Here, forget your worries. A young man like you shouldn't look so unhappy."

"How much?"

"Don't worry, this one is for free."

"And the catch is?"

"Catch? What is catch?"

"Nothing... just give me the booze."

Samuel began to drink. He was thirsty and managed to neck the entire pint.

"Feel better?"

"It's a good start," he replied, slamming the empty glass onto the bar.

"Maybe you like another?" and before Samuel had a chance to agree, she was pouring him a second pint.

"I didn't realize it was my birthday."

"I just felt a little sorry for you, that's all."

"I don't want your pity."

"Then maybe you pay for this one?"

He grinned, but only took a sip from the second pint.

"What is this stuff anyway?"

"Columbiana...You like it?"

"I like it a lot, could I have another?"

To his surprise she began to pour him a third.

"Probably best if I finish this one first."

She smiled.

"Take your time, there is no hurry."

"Say, don't you have a name? I think it's only right that I know your name."

"Rosanna...There you go young man."

The third pint was pressed carefully into Samuel's palm.

"Thanks Rosanna, you know what? I think somebody should give you an award, I honestly do."

"Oh, really?"

"Sure...The world's best barmaid, the very best!"

"That is a nice thing to know, and what is your name?"

"Samuel, Samuel Locke," he replied.

He was starting to feel dizzy and had struggled to think about the reply. As he drank, Rosanna watched him closely, both her elbows resting across the bar, her head cupped between her two hands. Her face now donned such a curious look;

it was as if Samuel had just said something very strange to her.

"You know, your drinks are pretty strong Rosanna."

"The strongest."

"Not even sure if I care about my father any more. I'm quite certain he didn't give two hoots about me," Samuel rambled on, his head growing lighter by the second. An uncomfortable thought then crossed his mind. He remembered a time in Paris, several years ago, when he'd sunk a bottle of absinthe. That stuff had nearly killed him, and he hoped now that this latest alcoholic experiment would not prove just as dangerous.

"Excuse me old man, but could I possibly snatch a light?"

Samuel swivelled to his left to find the card playing Westerner now standing next to him, a cigarette hanging limp between his two wrinkled forefingers.

"A light?" the man repeated. He spoke very precisely, with a posh accent and had become only the third Englishman that Samuel had met during his entire two months in Colombia.

"Sure, no problem," Samuel replied, beginning to fish about in his pockets.

"Got one here somewhere, pretty sure of that."

For some reason his fingers weren't working quite as well as they usually did and the harder he tried the more awkward they became.

"Need a hand there, young man?"

"No, no, I'm fine, just give me a second."

"Should watch that Columbiana Samuel, the locals all swear by it, but if you're not used to the stuff, it's liable to blow your bloody head off!"

Finally, Samuel managed to free the small silver lighter from his pocket and after two attempts she fired.

"Say, how did you know my name?" he asked, lighting the stranger's cigarette.

"I never gave you my name."

The Englishman took his first drag.

"I overheard you and Rosanna talking. Nothing untoward old man."

"Oh, forget I asked."

"Already forgotten, now I don't suppose you'd care for a game of cards? Only the friends who were with me have had to leave...Urgent business and all that."

"Cards? You know, I'm not really a gambling man," Samuel replied.

The truth was he loved to play cards, any game of cards, but the Columbiana had gone to his head so quick he was having serious trouble keeping his thoughts straight; a condition not best suited to playing cards.

"Now everybody gambles friend, in their own peculiar way...Perhaps just a quick game?"

"The thing is I was still talking to Rosanna..."

But Rosanna had gone. Samuel turned to find her, but she had simply vanished.

"Does everybody just disappear in this place?"

"You'd be surprised young man...Now what about that game of ours?"

"Game?"

"Our friendly game of cards. You told me you were pretty good."

"I did?"

"Of course you did."

Before he was able to collect his thoughts, Samuel found a firm arm wrapped about his shoulders, and was then gently ushered towards a table. Feeling uneasy, the handful of backpackers had long since gone, and now only the town's locals were present as Samuel took a seat amongst them.

"I thought you said your friends had left?"

"I have lots of friends Samuel...Poker?"

"Excuse me?"

"What game shall we play?" the stranger continued, expertly shuffling his deck. His hands were moving very quick and Samuel's heavy eyes were unable to keep up. Feeling suddenly queasy, he glanced towards the locals who sat with him. They each stared back, their faces expressionless, having seen many drunken Englishmen over the years and seeing nothing of any great interest in their latest guest.

"Having a good day guys?" Samuel spoke, unable to hide his sarcasm. No reply. Each of the men remained stoical, calmly studying their new arrival.

"Friendly bunch you got here."

"They don't speak much English Samuel...Remember you're in their country now," the Westerner spoke, beginning to deal the cards.

"Say, what school did you go to? You sound a little posh to me," Samuel continued.

"I went to Eton. What about yourself?"

"Princethorpe, I got sent to a place called Princethorpe, not on your level, but we had a killer rugby team all the same."

The toff stopped dealing. He now appeared genuinely intrigued with what Samuel had to say.

"Princethorpe? Sounds familiar."

"Wouldn't have thought so, only a minor public school, stuck right out in the sticks."

"Still, the name does ring a bell."

"If you say so."

"By the way, my name is Shelley, Sebastian Shelley," Samuel's new friend continued, leaning over to shake his hand. Samuel didn't even notice Rosanna taking a seat next to him until another glass of beer was shoved under his nose.

"Hey! Look whose back. You play cards too?"

She smiled. She didn't look so bad either now that he'd sank a few. Maybe if he could get his words out straight, the right kind of words, he'd have some fun later on.

"How you feel now Samuel?" Rosanna asked, her soothing tone still intact. Such a nice, soft voice. Just listening to that voice made Samuel feel even sleepier. Maybe he could lay down for a second and steal some rest.

"How you feel?" she continued.

"Like I just left an Irish wake," he replied, not quite sure what he was saying any more, and not being particularly bothered.

"Take another sip from your drink, you said you liked it."

"If it's all the same, I'd rather not."

"Better not to fight it, Samuel," Sebastian chipped in.

"Fight it? Fight what?"

"Take another sip Samuel, you'll like this drink even better, I promise," Rosanna continued, her smile still fixed.

"Hey! What's going on here?"

"Going on?" Sebastian replied, carefully placing the full deck of cards onto the table. By now Samuel could hardly see straight. In his growing panic he even grabbed the edge of his seat to keep himself upright. As he did, two of the locals leaned over and held him steady.

"Who the hell are you anyway?" Samuel then snapped, still facing Sebastian.

"I told you already, my name is Sebastian, Sebastian Shelley."

"Well it sounds like a girl's name to me Shelley...You some kind of girly?"

"How is your head Samuel?" Rosanna broke in.

Samuel tried to turn in her direction but only managed to fall from his chair. The two Colombians moved quickly to reseat him.

"You put something in my drink!"

"That's right Samuel, we did," she went on.

"But I don't understand, why you put some..." he wasn't able to get the last word out properly. His mouth felt numb, he couldn't feel his tongue either.

"Burundanga Samuel," Shelley continued.

"Bura what?"

"Burundanga...It's a drug, a useful weapon in this part of the world too. Very flexible. We can put it into almost anything you know: Sweets, cigarettes, chewing gum; even beer."

"But...Why?" Samuel just managed to ask.

"Because you've been asking all the wrong questions, young man."

"Questions? What..."

"You claim to be looking for a man named Jack Locke," Sebastian interrupted. By nature he was a very impatient man and could no longer wait for Samuel to find his words. Time was pressing and he had so much to do still, so much to worry over. The boy was holding things up.

"I am...He's...He's my father damn it!" Samuel then spluttered out.

"He came in here! I saw him!"

"So you say...I suppose we'll find out soon enough."

Samuel went to lunge at him, but with the Colombians holding him back, and with the drug starting to take its full effect, he could only struggle.

"Don't fight it Samuel, your life is not under threat. At least not yet. The drug will render you unconscious for a few hours, perhaps even a day, but it won't kill you, slight memory loss, but it won't kill you."

"I'm...I'm going to kill you damn it!"

"Let's not hear such careless talk, best to part on good terms. And if you are who you claim to be, well then, all the better."

Samuel slumped forward one final time, his head smacking hard against the table's rough edge.

"Will you take good care of the boy Sebastian?" Rosanna then spoke, looking a little worried as Samuel's mouth had begun to twitch.

"I think he is a nice boy," she finished.

"Now even nice boys can spread careless talk Rosanna," Sebastian answered, helping the Colombians to tie Samuel's limp hands together.

2

New In Town

Samuel could not remember cracking his head against the edge of the table. He'd long drifted off by the time his skull had met wood, and the dream world which he now inhabited could not have been further removed from the smoky, Colombian hotel bar that he'd recently stumbled into. In his dream Samuel Locke was now six. It was the end of his first day back at big school, and a day that he would never forget. It had been etched firmly into his memory.

He stood impatiently outside his tall, school gates in Bethnal Green, East London, waiting for his father to pick him up. It was getting late. It was cold too. He stood shivering, wearing a thin, black pair of short pants and a neatly pressed white shirt, his school tie having been stuffed into the satchel which was now slung across his shoulder. The other boys and girls in his year had already been collected by their parents and driven back home. Only some of the older students remained, and they were big enough to make their own way back on foot. He watched them wander off, laughing and joking together as they disappeared around the first bend in the long road. Watching them slip from view, he began to feel afraid. His dad would never forget to pick him up and it was already getting dark.

Samuel was beginning to think that his father was never going to show up, and had already decided to make his way back into the school; perhaps ask one of the nicer teachers to look after him until somebody at least remembered to pick him up when, just as he was turning towards the rusted gates, he spotted a long, black limousine cruising towards him down the main road.

"Dad," he whispered as the car approached.

His day at school had been a good one. He'd painted some very fine pictures of his house and couldn't wait to show his father who always seemed very pleased with what he was shown. The limousine pulled to a stop an inch or two from the kerb. Its back door flew open, and out jumped a tall, slender man in his early forties. Jack Locke boasted a thick mane of wild blonde hair, and when he'd bothered to shave, he could have passed for a man in his early thirties.

"Sammy boy!" he yelled, flinging wide both his arms and falling down onto one knee as his son raced towards him.

"And how have you been today young sir? Been working hard? Chasing those girls?"

"No way!" Samuel protested, pulling several crumpled pieces of paper from inside his shirt.

"And what do we have here then?"

Samuel showed his father the paintings.

"My word, an undiscovered masterpiece by Da Vinci himself! Tell me boy where did you come upon this, in some attic? How much will you be wanting for it, eh?"

"I painted it!"

"You did this! Well, I would never have guessed, a son of mine, so talented."

"It's our house."

"I knew that the second I looked at it, why you even gave us an extra set of windows, how very kind."

Samuel gave his dad a strong hug. It lasted several seconds, but by the time they parted the dream had already begun to take its turn for the worst. It had been Samuel who'd first spotted the approaching vehicles, noted the flashing blue lights long before those terrible sirens had begun to sound.

"Dad?"

"Don't you worry son."

In a matter of seconds both father and son were surrounded by a number of police cars and vans.

"What's happening dad? What do they want?"

The vehicle doors burst open and a dozen or so armed police jumped out.

"Dad!"

Jack stayed silent. He didn't put up a fight. For the sake of his son, who he loved dearly, he didn't once protest as the officers moved in to cuff him.

"Be careful with the boy, you hear?" was the only request that Jack made as they led him away into one of the vans. Samuel tried to follow, but a young police officer had already wrapped his arms tightly about his waist. There was nothing he could do except watch as his father was bundled into the back of the police van and then driven away at high speed, the terrible wailing sound again ringing in his ears. He couldn't have known it at the time, but that would be the last he would see of his father for many years to come.

"You okay there lad?" the young officer had spoken, loosening his grip somewhat. Samuel had not replied, his eyes still fixed on the police van which grew smaller and smaller as each second passed. He would not speak for many days to come, not even to his own mother when she'd arrived at the police station to take him home.

"Please, no more booze..." Samuel continued to mumble, half awake, but with a vague awareness that he was once again a living, breathing part of the real world. His dream was already fading. The police vans with their flashing lights, once perfectly vivid in his mind's eye, had now become but distant flecks in a vast ocean of blackness. For a long period of time he did his very best to maintain the various images, but it was no use, the dream had gone.

Almost fully conscious, his body began to shift, and each time it did a terrible, stinging pain, which seemed to pinch every inch of his skin, steadily intensified. Perversely, Samuel pictured himself lying flat and naked at the very heart of some boundless desert, and only when he began to hear the sound of many children at play, close by, did he force his sleepy eyes to open.

The intense glare from the sun high above momentarily blinded him, and it took some time before his vision was able to adjust itself properly. His surroundings had dramatically changed. There was no sign of the hotel, or even the narrow street where he'd found the hotel. All this had gone. It was early morning too, a bright, scorching start to the day.

He was lying half naked at the centre of what looked like a large town square. Gently raising his head from the ground, he was in time to watch a group of scruffy children running away from him, at full pelt across this square, one of them holding onto his shirt and letting it blow wildly behind him as he ran.

Tentatively, Samuel put a hand to his exposed, and now sunburnt chest, winced violently at the pain which followed and began to groan. He'd experienced bad days before, but nothing quite like this. He felt weak. He felt dizzy too, and without a drink soon he knew he would only pass out again. His eyes began to roam the square. It sat empty except for the children and a few other figures who scuttled hither and tither at its outer limits.

With some force of effort, he managed to haul himself slowly onto his elbows. Something light brushed against the side of his face as he did. Glancing skyward, he found himself sitting beneath the branches of a tall tree, each branch draped in several long, silvery tillandsium fronds, so that a spectacular transparent curtain of foliage appeared to hang over him.

The surrounding town looked small. He was no longer in Doncella either. He was sure of that. Doncella had been a dirty slum. This new town, wherever it was, looked relatively clean. Small whitewashed buildings encircled the square. Beyond these he could see many others, only brighter, multi-coloured.

Feeling exhausted, he let himself rest against the trunk of the tree, his eyes returning to the long, silvery tillandsium fronds, and to the peculiar way in which they were each made to glitter as the sun's strong rays danced through them. He cast his tired mind back to the hotel, back to Sebastian and the barmaid who'd spiked his drink. Had her name been Rosanna? He could see their faces clearly, could see their mouths opening and closing as they spoke, but could hear no words. He watched as Sebastian dealt out his pack of cards. One, two, three they fell before his sweaty fingers, each one boasting a picture of the grim reaper!

Had he really seen his father slipping into the hotel? He tried to recall the precise moment when he'd first spotted the familiar looking old man wandering in amongst Doncella's bustling crowds, but found his brain simply too tired for such a strenuous task. Instead, he closed his eyes, and before he knew it, he'd once again fallen asleep.

~ ~ ~

Maria Quintana strolled into the town's main square at five minutes past seven, twenty minutes after her latest shift at work had ended. She was not in the best of moods either. She was never to be found in a good mood so soon after finishing work. Maria hated her job. She worked in the town's largest and most popular strip joint, and although she was the club's most popular dancing girl, the admiration she garnered did nothing to wash away her disgust for the occupation.

That evening's shift had been a bad one, perhaps the worst since she'd started there three years previous. The small town of Sevilla was poor, had always been poor, and yet almost every punter who'd paid good money to see her strip that evening had somehow found the cash to pay for a private dance too. And those were the worst.

In spite of this she worked hard at upholding her dignity. Where the other girls would sometimes allow their clients a secret caress, Maria kept a healthy distance. She maintained a fixed smile; simple reasons enough perhaps for why she'd become so popular over the years. A firm line had been drawn. All of the men knew it, and all of them wanted to cross it first.

It was Sunday morning. The church bells were ringing, calling the locals to mass. As she watched the people streaming towards the church, some of whom she recognized from her previous night of entertaining, she took a seat at one of the many benches which ringed the square. She often did this the morning after a particularly bad evening, and today would be no different. If she attracted the occasional glance of disapproval from the passing Christians, she ignored it. Over the past few years she'd become good at ignoring other people's accusing eyes, their opinions, and of course her own feelings. What did it matter what other people thought of her? Nothing. They all had their secrets, dirty, unmentionable secrets, just like her.

She sat on the bench watching the self-righteous throng pass by, some dragging children in tandem, all dressed in their best clothes, and thought to herself what a terrible sight it was too. It was then, as her temper began to rise, she noticed the figure of a young man sprawled out beneath the square's only tree. The sun was strong that morning. He didn't seem to be wearing a shirt, and more out of curiosity than any compassion she began a slow walk over towards him.

He wasn't Colombian that was for certain. His skin was too pale, too freckled. He was maybe European, but most likely just another American with too much dollar in his pocket and not enough sense to know how to hide it. She hovered over him and only when she saw how red his once pale chest had turned, did she begin to feel any genuine concern for the stranger.

"Hey you, wake up!"

Samuel could hear the distant voice calling to him but chose to ignore it. At that moment in time being asleep felt a better option than being awake; as being awake could only lead to more pain and more uncertainties.

"Time to get up now," the voice continued, a strong female voice.

A second later he felt a sharp kick to the stomach.

"You here what I say down there?"

Immediately his eyes flew open and now his hands, startled into action, tried in vain to grab the offending boot. No use. Whoever it was kept their safe distance.

"You speak English? I speak a little English."

Overhead, the long, silvery tillandsium fronds were still present, but now a new object mingled in amongst them, an object of some curiosity too.

"You okay?" the girl asked, her fine, dark hair almost touching his face as she hovered over him.

She looked tired. Deep shades of grey nestled beneath her lids. She was no great beauty, but neither was she plain. A combination of delicate features made her attractive: High cheek bones; a small nose and perfectly rounded lips. But above everything else it was her eyes that were her finest asset. Samuel thought they were the most wonderful light green and yet, he sensed, troubled by some secret sorrow that somehow only went to add to her appeal. She carried with her, her own peculiar brand of melancholy, some would say reserve, but as is the case with most such people, Samuel found himself drawn towards her rather than repelled. She was perhaps in her late twenties, and yet her skin, despite the late nights, looked so well preserved she could, at a glance, have appeared ten years younger.

"You speak English?" she repeated, her tone growing quite stern. Samuel feared that she was readying to leave and the idea of being left stranded in a strange town, for a second time, no longer appealed.

"I am English," he eventually replied, struggling to upright. It wasn't easy. He still felt half drugged and had taken his time.

"I think perhaps you should keep off the beer in future," she went on, flicking a few strands of hair quickly behind her right ear.

"Where am I?"

"You don't even know where you are?"

"Well, I wouldn't be asking otherwise," he snapped, surprised by his own short temper. The girl paused, perhaps wondering if the guy at her feet was really worth any of her attention after all.

"This is Sevilla, you know Sevilla?"

Samuel shook his head. He barely knew Colombia.

"You really should keep off the drink friend."

"I was drugged!"

The girl smiled.

"I know many drunks and even they lie better than you."

"Well, I'm afraid it's the truth," Samuel went on, not really caring if the girl believed him or not, just content that she was there at all.

"What is your name anyway lobster?" she asked, now kneeling next to him.

"Lobster?"

"Take a look yourself, you are just as red."

For a second time, Samuel glanced down at his raw, sunburnt chest.

"Bloody kids, they stole my shirt."

"I think maybe your drinking friends from last night stole it, no?"

"I told you I was drugged damn it!" he again snapped. He'd bought the shirt one Christmas in New York, his very favourite.

"Careful friend, don't shout at me, I can always leave," Maria replied. Samuel could see she was serious and managed to control his temper. What did she expect? She could see he was in a bad

36

way. Some understanding might have been better.

"I think I need a little help."

Maria nodded.

"I need to get to a telephone," he continued, trying to sound as harmless as possible. It seemed to work. Slowly, Maria's expression softened.

"I think you need some water first. You feel sick?"

Samuel shrugged.

"Just a little."

"And you're not some crazy guy who wants to kill me? I meet enough of them at work."

"Not sure I'd have the energy."

"I guess you don't look so dangerous."

"I'm not," Samuel replied, very softly for effect.

"Then I hope I don't regret this."

Without any further hesitation, Maria slipped her right arm around Samuel's painful chest, and slowly, with not a small amount of effort on both their parts, helped him to his feet.

"Where do we go now?" Samuel asked, the sunburn still causing him to wince periodically.

"Back to my place."

"You know, I'm not sure I caught your name."

"Maria Quintana...And you?"

"Samuel, plain old Samuel."

3

Mad, Bad And Dangerous To Know

Raul Morales stuck another bottle of Columbiana into his mouth. Not far below him, a second cock fight was just getting under way. He sat in his favourite high chair which overlooked the fighting pit, deciding how much he would bet on the third contest and if there was any possibility of being able to fix it.

In one month's time Raul would turn fifty. He was aware that people still feared him in town, their nervous glances and their way of being overtly nice to him while in his presence told him that, but his wilder days of kicking ass, anyone's ass, were rapidly drawing to their close. Too much booze and far too much coke were to blame for this decline, and these days Raul's one remaining ambition was simply to make enough cash to retire on before old age set in for good.

He let the empty bottle of Columbiana slip through his chubby, cigarette stained fingers and smash to the ground. It often depressed him when he thought of his earlier years, how fit and trim his body had once been. Fat and bloated was now most people's honest opinion if they were asked, and more often than not Raul relied on past reputation to get what he wanted from Seville's locals. It was better that way, better than to risk humiliation in front of so many people. Of course he had powerful friends too. Before he'd settled in Sevilla he'd grown cocoa plants in Caquetá for the rebel army, and they were always good for a favour. As a much younger man he'd even fought for them.

As the cock fight began, Raul left the comfort of his chair and bustled his way to the edge of the fighting pit. Out of respect, people cleared a path for him. He might have been turning fifty but at six foot four, he still towered above the majority of those who had gathered to see blood spilt that evening. A few even patted his broad back as he passed.

Raul was good at making money, lots and lots of money and usually in very short periods of time. These days he kidnapped rich, foreign backpackers, and although he'd recently learnt of competition in the form of one Jack Locke, an Englishman of all things, he felt there were still enough rich pickings to go around for everybody in town. He could see no point in making a fuss.

Raul wanted a nice, quiet life from now on; with Maria by his side, and God help anyone who tried to stop him. As long as this Jack Locke kept his operation discreet, then he was happy.

"Ah come on, can't you peck any harder?" Raul now yelled as the cocks fought one another. For a large man he owned a surprisingly soft voice and on numerous occasions, when in close company, he would find himself mumbling and having to repeat past sentences. He found this embarrassing and it often pushed him into an irritable mood.

The surrounding crowds continued to cheer, easily drowning out Raul's voice. It was all too much for one lonely figure. Leopold Balboni stood in the far corner of the underground den. He stood alone, immersed in shadow where he felt most comfortable; watching the screaming mob as they in turn overlooked the feathered battle before them.

Leopold wasn't feeling very good that morning. He was nervous, very nervous, and whenever his nerves got the better of him he would throw up. That morning alone he'd thrown up a record four times! Now his stomach ached, and the back of his throat felt very sore. He would have bought himself a bottle of throat medicine, but he'd as yet to find a pharmacy in Sevilla.

Leopold was nervous for one very good reason. He'd screwed up big time. The previous night, having left the strip club where he'd enjoyed the company of several pretty girls, all paid for, he'd spotted a young man crashed out in the main square whilst on his way home. Ordinarily, he would have stopped. It was his job to stop and run a curious eye over any potential hostage, but instead he'd stumbled back to his dingy flat much the worse for drink.

He should have checked the fella out. He should have checked him out knowing that finding a solitary western drunk in Colombia, if his family were wealthy enough, could make a lot of people an awful lot of money, and all in a relatively short space of time. Kidnapping was a thriving business and when it came to making big bucks you couldn't beat it.

Now Leopold was in a great deal of trouble. No amount of fast talking would get him out of it either. He'd ignored the young man. He'd simply walked by and sure enough, given time, Raul would find out and want to kill him. It was in moments like these that Leopold wished he'd listened to his friends and stayed put in New York.

"Boss, we need to talk boss," Leopold spoke, having found enough courage at last to leave the shadows and tell Raul himself. Maybe he would go easier on him?

"Boss?"

Raul chose to ignore him, like he often did. The fight was nearing its climax, and he wasn't going to miss its outcome because of a cockroach like Leopold. He could wait until it was all over.

"Boss, we really need to talk."

"Get lost little cockroach, I'm busy," Raul replied.

"But Raul this is very important, I think you should listen," Leopold went on, his short, scrawny body quivering.

"I'm going to lose my temper in a second Leopold, please don't push me."

"But..."

Raul spun around and grabbed the skinny New Yorker by the throat.

"Why is it that you never learn huh? Americans! How the hell did you all get to be so powerful?" the huge Colombian yelled.

Leopold was quickly turning blue.

"I think I strap a blade to your beak and throw you in with the chickens...Tell me Leopold, who do you think would win?"

Leopold shrugged. It was all he could do as he watched the gambling den turn black. Not wanting the hassle of yet another tricky body disposal, Raul loosened his grip and allowed Leopold, now gasping for breath, to collapse into a heap across the floor. For good measure, he then gave his assistant a solid kick to the stomach.

"Now get up cockroach, I haven't finished with you yet."

Very slowly, Leopold lifted his weary body from the floor.

"So what is it Leopold? What is so important?"

Leopold froze, glancing towards the noisy gamblers who still cheered on the vicious cockfight. A big part of Leopold now wanted to run headlong into that baying mob, lose himself completely, but fear kept him cemented.

"Well?" Raul persisted, his frustration beginning to build. Leopold could always tell when his boss was going to explode because his right eye would begin to twitch. He took a precautionary step back. The eye was having spasms.

"I won't ask you again cockroach."

"Last night, on my way home, I found someone."

"A foreigner?"

Nervously, Leopold nodded.

"So where is he now?" Raul continued, already second guessing the reply.

"I wasn't feeling well Raul, please..."

Raul grabbed the cockroach about the throat for a second time.

"Your job is so simple Leopold. You find me foreigners; then you come and fetch me...What could be so difficult?"

Again Leopold was turning blue.

"I'm sorry Boss, real sorry," he replied, only just able to form the words.

"You're always sorry Leopold, but you keep screwing up, I'd hold you hostage only your old ass wouldn't earn me a dime!"

The crowd behind them suddenly roared. Raul dropped Leo to the floor in time to see his hen being hacked to pieces.

"You see what bad luck you bring me Leopold?"

"Should I go back to the square Raul?" Leopold continued, both hands now rubbing at his neck.

"I think so, only this time I come with you," Raul replied.

With the crowds still cheering, both men left the gambling den.

~ ~ ~

After leaving the main square, Samuel was led at a leisurely pace through a maze of narrow alleyways, heading for Maria's flat. At one point during their journey Maria had stopped to knock on the door of a friend. The door had opened and Maria had disappeared inside leaving Samuel propped against the wall of the house. Five minutes later she had re-appeared, only this time holding onto a shirt she had borrowed from her friend's husband. Carefully folding the garment, she'd placed it into her handbag.

"It should fit you," she'd then spoke, wrapping her arm back around Samuel's waist, being careful not to catch his sunburn, and continuing up Sevilla's narrow, twisting streets. Whilst Maria had been inside her friend's house Samuel had considered leaving her and setting off on his own. It was a reckless thought but it had occurred to him that he may have been walking into some sort of ambush.

He knew all about Colombia's reputation for kidnapping. Even his editor back in London, who'd never had much time for him, had warned against traveling across country while in Colombia alone. If the rebel army didn't get hold of you then the drug smugglers probably would. Either way there was a fair chance of being taken hostage and, in Colombia, the ransoms were expected to be paid. It was a business, pure and simple. If your family refused to pay up, well, you wouldn't get to see them again. So Samuel had put his faith in the girl, had given her permission to take care of him, and after a further twenty minutes walking, they had reached her flat.

~ ~ ~

"How does that feel Samuel?"

Samuel smiled into the huge pillow. He'd taken stupid risks all his life, even as a child. Sometimes they paid off, sometimes they didn't. As Maria sat next to him on her bed, her soft hands gently running up and down his torso, he felt he'd got lucky once again.

"The cream, it feel cold?" she continued.

Samuel wasn't thinking about the cream. He'd been single for far too long, and had almost forgotten how good a pair of female hands could feel. He smiled.

"No...The cream feels just fine Maria."

"You will be sore for a long time I think."

"It's getting better though."

She squeezed another dollop of soothing cream into the palm of her hand and then rubbed it slowly into his chest.

"You came to a bad town, Samuel."

"It wasn't my intention believe me."

"For an Englishman like you it can be very dangerous here."

"I'll take my chances, besides I'm not planning to stick around for long."

Long enough to track down his father. Only then would he leave.

"But why you come to Colombia anyway? So far away from home."

"I guess my work brought me here."

"Work? What is your work?"

"Oh, I take snaps...Nothing special."

"It sounds like fun, and your father, why is he here?"

Samuel paused. That was a very good question.

"I have no idea, but if I know my father he'll be up to no good."

"Maybe that is why his friends get rid of you, maybe he does not want to be found," she went on, now working her hands into the base of his neck where the sun had also taken hold.

"I think you could be right there Maria," he replied, his thoughts once more focusing on Jack, Maria's tender caresses almost forgotten.

"Your father sounds very interesting, I would like to meet him one day," she finished, running a concerned eye over his body.

Maria wouldn't be alone either. Samuel knew there were plenty of other people back home who'd been chasing Jack for years, eager for their own private little chat: People he'd managed to rip off, friends of people he'd had beaten up. They were all out there, simply dying to catch up.

"And what about yourself? If this town is so rotten, why do you stay here?"

Maria stopped rubbing the cream into his skin and turned her head away. Samuel sat himself up.

"Maria?"

"I think the less you know about me, the better Samuel."

"Why? What do you do that's so bad?"

"Please. Don't play stupid. You can see the sort of clothes I wear."

Glancing about her room, Samuel could see the many photos of her friends too, pinned against the dilapidated walls. They were strippers. Just like her.

"Well, dancing for a living isn't so bad. Besides, you sound like a smart girl. Save some cash. Skip town."

"You don't understand. It's not so simple for me. And honey, I do more than just dance," she calmly replied, leaving the bed and placing the half emptied tube of cream onto her dresser.

Samuel decided not to pry any further. It was her business. Nothing to do with him.

"I take a bath now. You can stay a few hours, but then you go."

"Go, go where?"

"Not my problem," she replied, beginning to unzip her skirt.

"Could I not stay the night? I'll sleep in the chair, I wouldn't be a problem," he spoke, watching her skirt slip to the floor. Underneath, she wore a tiny black thong, and he had to struggle to keep his eyes on hers.

"My boyfriend lives here too Samuel. I don't think he'd like to share."

"Boyfriend?"

She pointed to a framed picture which lay on a small table next to her bed. A large, tough looking Colombian; a thick arm wrapped across Maria's shoulder, could be seen within the frame. Samuel didn't like the look of him.

"You have enough cash?" Maria continued, pulling her tight, red blouse free from over her head. Samuel looked away, surprised by his own coyness.

"Well?" He fumbled around in his back pocket and pulled out a crumpled fifty dollar bill.

"Just about."

"Then you go back to the main square, there is a bus which leaves for Santa Marta tonight. I think you should be on it."

"And in the meantime?"

She undid her bra.

"You sound like a smart boy Samuel, I'm sure you'll think of something," she replied, turning quickly and stepping into the adjacent bathroom, its door shut firmly the second she was inside. For a time he listened to the sound of running bath water. There can be days, he thought, when your luck just runs out.

4

Mr. Sebastian Shelley

Up until Sevilla, Leopold Balboni had spent most of his years scrounging out a living in New York, and a larger part of them behind bars. Addiction had been his downfall. Addiction to anything really. Leopold had never been fussy in that respect. You name it, he'd probably given it a go: heroin, cocaine, whores. He'd revelled in them all, and so coming to Colombia, after ripping off the local hardware store, had been one of the easiest decisions of his sordid life so far.

Leopold was not a clever man. If anyone could have been accused of being ignorant, it was him. Fifty six years of life had taught him little. When he'd first thought of going to South America, Colombia in particular, he'd thought of a paradise; a home away from home, a place where the women and the drugs were dirt cheap; and although this was pretty much close to the truth,

Leopold had simply chosen to ignore all those people who'd warned him against going to a country which stood on the brink of collapse.

He wouldn't hear a bad word said against his paradise, and like the fool he was, he'd left New York early one autumn with a few hundred dollars stuffed into his pocket, and a bagful of old clothes slung over his shoulder. Leopold had stumbled into Sevilla late one evening. He'd found the nearest strip club and planted himself down in front of the girls, content to drink the night away. He'd struck up a conversation with Raul, the club's owner, not long after midnight. The pair had got on famously, just as Raul had hoped, and from that moment on, Leopold's fate had been sealed. His paradise would quickly turn into a hell, and there wouldn't be a lot he could do about it. By the end of their first month, Raul already had him hooked on crack.

Leopold now wandered aimlessly about the edge of the main square. The stranger had vanished and Raul, having quickly grown bored of searching, had gone back to his strip club. By the time he'd left, Leopold was feeling hungry. He was feeling sorry for himself too, wondering just how it was that he'd allowed himself to get caught up with a drug smuggler, kidnapper and occasional murderer when, from across the square, he spotted Samuel walking towards him.

Like the large but agile rat that he was, Leopold quickly ducked into the nearest alleyway.

He wouldn't screw up this time. He couldn't afford to. The job as he saw it was simple enough. He'd find out all he could about the stranger, and then report it back to Raul. At that point he could relax.

Samuel had found his way to the main square easily enough. Maria did not live far, and with all Sevilla's streets seemingly leading towards the busy central plaza, it had taken him no longer than thirty minutes. In the end, Maria had let him rest at her flat for several hours. As he'd left, it had turned eight. Now the sun had begun to set and people were streaming into the plaza from all over town. Samuel loitered for a while near the square centre, watching them arrive. He still had the crumpled fifty dollar note in his back pocket and before he did anything else, he wanted to sink a couple of cool beers. It was still warm and most of the male locals who passed him by wore little more than flimsy vests; all they could afford. Samuel chose one of the lively salsa bars which ringed the main square, anxious to blend, and perhaps then figure out the previous night's events.

Jack Locke was here, somewhere. That much he was certain of. It was only a matter of time before he made his presence felt, and Samuel was in no great hurry to leave. The salsa bar looked packed. As he neared, a crowd of people outside were busy lighting fireworks. He looked to the hills which rose above the town, lush, green hills;

each of them rising in stark contrast against the tiny white buildings which they observed. He began to picture the evening's light, grey sky suddenly awash in brilliant multi-coloured explosions as the fireworks were lit. He took his time approaching. He was in no hurry. He noticed some people wearing fancy dress, and was trying to pin down the exact festival when a strangely familiar voice called out to him.

"Mr. Locke."

To his immediate right the crowds had parted. A single reveller remained, watching him closely, his face obscured by a peculiar feathered mask. Nevertheless Samuel recognized him. It wasn't difficult. The drug he'd been given the previous night had not completely wiped his memory.

Along with the mask, the stranger wore a tatty white shirt and a pair of black shoes, now so old and worn that he might have been better off wearing nothing at all. Hadn't he called himself Shelley?

"Samuel Locke?"

"Shelley..."

"Follow me Mr. Locke please," the Englishman continued, turning briskly away from Samuel and heading just as briskly into the crowds.

Samuel followed. At least he did his best to follow. As he pushed his way forward, dozens of people, still arriving, began to swell around him. Shelley was quite short, and quite nimble too, and Samuel soon lost sight of his prey. Eventually, he managed to navigate the crowds and found himself facing a long flight of steps which snaked their way up the side of a small cafe bar.

Here, at the very top of the staircase, stood Shelley. He looked rather impatient, and even managed to roll his eyes at Samuel's belated appearance.

"Timekeeping really isn't your thing, is it Samuel?"

"I'm going to kill you Shelley," Samuel barked. He would too, just as soon as he caught his breath.

"Oh, do hurry up; we have more important matters to discuss. Your father really isn't happy with you at all!" came the almost casual reply. Incensed, Samuel hauled himself up the steps. At their summit he hoped to find Shelley and his father.

"Well, that was quick," Shelley quipped as Samuel reached the top.

A wide rooftop fell away before him. A small whitewashed table and two chairs sat in its centre.

"Please, sit down," Shelley continued, gently patting one of the seats.

"Screw you."

Jack was nowhere to be seen, but still Shelley was not alone. Soon after Samuel had reached the rooftop, he'd felt the cool tip of a pistol pressed against his head. The skinny Colombian kid who held it could have been no more than twenty.

"Don't you fight your own battles Shelley?" Samuel asked, his eyes still fixed on the well-spoken English gent who stood some distance away, beside the balcony railings.

"Mario, they'll be no need for violence, Mr. Locke isn't a stupid man," the reply came.

"You sure boss?"

"I'm sure."

Slowly, the gun was removed. Samuel threw the trigger happy Colombian an evil glance before following Shelley over towards the railings.

"I expect you're after some sort of apology?" Shelley began as Samuel reached him.

"Amongst other things."

Shelley's cool was still intact which only made Samuel even angrier. Just one good punch. That was all he asked, and then he'd find Jack.

"My name is Sebas..."

"Sebastian Shelley, I remember."

The shorter man held out his hand, but Samuel declined the offer. His fists were still tightly clenched, and it was a struggle to keep his temper in check.

"You mentioned my father."

"That's right, I did," Shelley replied, grinning. A brilliant flash of light burst overhead, followed by the sound of thunder. Samuel flinched. Shelley in contrast remained calm, turning slowly from Samuel to study the square and its people down below.

"Such a vibrant country Colombia. Any excuse to throw a party. Not like in England. I love it here. I really do."

"You've known my father long?"

"I've known your father all my life, my closest friend. We used to run all the best rackets in London you know. I expect you don't remember London. Would have been too young. Three perhaps?"

"I was six, and no, I don't remember London much. I must have blanked it. Something bad happened to me in London."

"It wasn't easy for Jack either."

"Screw Jack!"

Shelley walked calmly towards a table and two chairs where a bottle of wine and two glasses had been set out for them.

"Drink?"

"Not right now, the local tipple goes straight to my head."

Shelley chuckled, pouring himself a glass.

"Yes, quite, we really should apologize for that one. Still, it was important to have you checked out. You were asking a lot of difficult questions."

"I had too, my father's a tricky man. Takes a lot of effort to pin him down."

"But a wonderful man Samuel, a wonderful man."

A second set of fireworks exploded overhead. Down below, the music had been pumped up to full blast; and now Samuel and Shelley had to shout if either hoped to hear one another.

"What the hell is going on Shelley?" Samuel continued, taking a step closer towards Sebastian, conscious of the Colombian kid who still watched his every move.

"All quite simple really."

"Care to elaborate?"

Shelley took a slow sip from his glass; cast his eyes back over the balcony.

"We're running a little scam over here."

"I'd gathered that much."

"We borrow people Samuel."

"Borrow?"

"Borrow, kidnap. It's all the same really, just as long as we get paid."

"You kidnap people...What people?"

"Students, mostly. We like to borrow rich American students on their travels. It's all quite simple and quite brilliant."

"You're both crazy!"

"Possibly, but still, we can make a bundle of cash doing it."

Samuel paused, trying to take in everything that was being said. He'd known of his father's previous scams back in England, but kidnapping genuinely surprised him.

"Still, it's not all rosy; we have the other lot to consider too."

"What other lot?"

Shelley quickly necked his glass of wine. Beneath the mask, his piggy little eyes narrowed.

"The rebels. The FARC to be exact. They don't like to share. Especially large amounts of cash. Doesn't look good. Sends out the wrong message."

"The rebels..." Samuel whispered. Perhaps this time his father really had bitten off more than he could chew.

"So you see, you're in a lot of danger young man. Your father knows you are here, but he wants shot of you."

"I'm not leaving town until I've seen him," Samuel replied, adamant.

"Not your choice. You're lucky we decided to tell you this much. We could have shipped you off to Brazil if we'd wanted too. Now there's a bus which leaves for Santa Marta tonight from the main square. We expect to see you on it," Shelley spoke, placing the empty glass back onto the table.

"I'm not leaving town until I've seen my father Shelley, to hell with your bus!" Shelley turned casually away, and started for the stairwell.

"Shelley!"

"Tonight Mr. Locke. Tonight!"

Samuel couldn't control his temper any longer. He raced across the rooftop and grabbed Shelley by the arm. He would have strangled him too but for the gun which was again pressed into his skull.

"I kill 'im now?"

"Put the gun down Mario."

"But boss."

"Mario!"

Reluctantly, Mario removed the pistol for a second time.

"I want to see him Shelley."

"He doesn't want to see you."

"Then make him damn it! Talk to him!"

Shelley and Mario started down the stairwell.

"Tonight Mr. Locke! Tonight please!"

~ ~ ~

Maria was opening the door to her flat when she spotted Raul turning the corner at the far end of her street. She didn't wait to watch him start running. She threw herself into her hallway, but wasn't quick enough to lock the door.

"Get out!"

"What? No kiss?" Raul spoke, his bear like frame already halfway inside the flat.

"I said get out!" Maria continued, pushing all of her weight against the door. It was no match, and it wasn't long before Raul was standing tall inside her tiny room, holding her by the neck; his choice grip.

"Is that anyway to talk to your loving boyfriend?"

Maria spat in his face. In turn, Raul flung her across the bed.

"Never learn do you baby?"

"I told you, we're finished!"

"Only I can decide when we're over, not you, understood?" he snapped, beginning to cast a critical eye over the flat. He didn't like what he saw. The place was a mess. Across the floor, Maria had thrown her clothes into several untidy piles. He kicked at them as he wandered the room.

"You always were the untidy bitch."

"This is my place, I do what I like."

"And how do you earn the cash to pay for this place eh?"

Maria leapt from the bed and began to punch Raul's barrel chest. Each of her fragile strikes made little impact however.

"Get out!"

Raul grabbed her arms; drawing her into him.

"Together we could make a lot of money baby, don't you want that?"

"I'd never see a single dollar."

Raul grinned. She spoke the truth.

"I can't afford to lose you Maria; you're my best dancing girl. The club would be lost without you."

"Then find someone else. There are plenty of other poor girls like me in Colombia."

"No, not like you...None of them would be like you," he whispered, pushing her back onto the bed.

"Times are tough. I need you to stick around for a while."

"To hell with you!"

He sighed, turning to face the window.

"Always the same. Always confrontation…You know there was a time when we were close, a time when you were happy to walk by my side,"

"I was never happy Raul…I stayed with you out of fear. Nothing more. I could never love a pig like you."

Still facing the window, Raul began to shake his head slowly. She was lying. In his mind's eye he could picture them together, hand in hand, strolling through Sevilla. It was no trick of the imagination. He could still see the smile on her face. Quickly facing her, he pulled something free from his shirt pocket.

"Here, I bought you this. It's your favourite colour."

The tiny yellow blouse landed across her lap. With a quick flick of her wrist, it was thrown to the floor, at once hidden amongst the other clothes which lived there.

"I thought you could wear it tonight, I thought it would make you happy. I do try to make you happy."

"Keep your cheap gifts Raul; you don't have what I want."

"Can't we just be friends Maria? If only for one night. I get so very tired fighting like this."

Leaving the bed, she walked calmly over to where Raul stood, her face almost touching the tip of his chin as she stopped.

"Then you'd better make the most of it, because one day I'll be gone...I'll be out this stinking dump!"

Wearily, Raul smiled.

"Not on your wages baby...Not this lifetime."

5

Guardian Angel

After his meeting with Shelley, Samuel had hit the nearest salsa bar. Now, some two hours later, his head felt light as he stumbled outside. To hell with Shelley and to hell with the bus. He'd find his father regardless. Sevilla looked like a small town and Jack Locke didn't suit small towns. People always talked and it was only a matter of time before he picked up on a lead.

Tripping over his third kerb in less than two minutes, Samuel decided to give up on his search, at least until he was sober, and allowed himself to collapse into the nearest alleyway. Fortunately, several crates of rotting fruit broke his fall. Lifting his head, he could see that the narrow alleyway rose gently out of sight.

As he'd landed amongst the rotting fruit, a young kitten, having been feasting upon the same remains, suddenly took fright and darted across the alleyway's dusty cobblestones, diving headlong into the nearest open doorway. Several hanging beads of varying colours covered this doorway. From within the building, a low light burned, and as Samuel, still very much bleary eyed, studied the swaying beads, he listened contentedly to the music which also emanated from within. He could hear jazz; he was certain despite the ringing in his ears.

There was no salsa music being played here. Chet Baker was the order of the day. He was beginning to hum along when a tall figure appeared behind the beads. Samuel thought he noticed a grubby white suit, fading black shoes. The figure remained where he was; watching him.

"Dad...?"

Unable to carry Samuel's weight any longer, the crates shattered beneath him. He fell from the pile headfirst onto the cobblestones. For a split second, the stranger behind the beads went to help him, but froze. Again, lifting his head clear of the cobblestones, Samuel called out:

"Jack Locke? Is that you I see, Jack Locke? Hiding from your own flesh and blood! That's a terrible thing to do. Not afraid are we Jack?"

"You drunk again?" a soft voice from above sounded.

Slowly, ever so slowly, Samuel looked up.

"You still here?"

He smiled, a goofy grin.

"Maria! You know, I was just coming to see you."

She stood with her arms crossed, her hair neatly tied back. Her face was covered in so much make-up he almost didn't recognize her. He could see that she was far from happy though; her expression perfectly stern as she glared down at him.

"Well, you look real nice. You come to take me out Maria?"

"I start my work in twenty minutes, Samuel."

"And what does your boyfriend think about your work?"

"My boyfriend is none of your concern."

"Tell me Maria, does he beat you often?"

Automatically, her hand moved to the side of her face where a large bruise was still visible.

"My mother used to wear make-up too. Lots of the stuff. Still, it didn't always hide the marks. Like to know what I did to her boyfriend?" Samuel went on.

Feeling self-conscious, Maria quickly turned her face away.

"There's a bus which..."

"...Which leaves from the town centre. I know!" Samuel snapped.

"Well, you're going to miss it."

"Screw the bus."

"That your final word?"

"You bet."

"Then fine, I wish you all the luck," she replied, beginning to walk.

Samuel quickly scrambled to his feet. A few uneven strides later and he was by her side.

"Maria, wait, I didn't mean to shout like that."

"Leave me alone, I don't talk to stinking drunks."

"But I'm not drunk, just a little merry is all."

Maria continued to walk and continued to ignore the drunk.

"Ah, come on Maria, I've had a real hard day, can't you give me a break?"

No reply.

"Damn it, don't ignore me!" Samuel barked, grabbing her by the arm and pulling her to a swift stop. As he did, she spun around and slapped him as hard as she could across the face. Immediately, he let go.

"Jesus!"

"Don't you ever touch me like that again, you got that?"

"Sorry...I..."

"And please, don't say sorry. It is weak!"

"I just wanted to talk, Christ! I thought girls like to communicate?"

"It's not safe to talk here, not in a town like this, not for a guy like you, don't you get it yet?"

"I think I'm starting to see the picture."

"Don't miss that bus Samuel. It could be your last chance."

"You know, it sure feels like everybody in this town wants shot of me."

"Then maybe you should start listening to them."

"Oh, really?"

"Yes, really," she replied, softly.

"Well in that case Maria, have a nice life," he continued, beginning to walk away, heading for the nearest kerb.

"Samuel...Wait." He continued a few paces, and then stopped.

"What now?"

"Just a question."

"Haven't you said enough already?" he went on, his hand still toying with that side of his face where Maria had slapped him.

"I just wanted to know...You find your Papa?"

He glanced back towards the empty doorway. As expected, the figure had gone; the music too had died, only the kitten remained, attacking the beads with its paws.

"No...I didn't find my father," he eventually replied.

"Perhaps this was for the best?"

"Sure, perhaps it was."

"I have to work now Samuel. You, you make sure you catch your bus, Si?"

"Whatever you say Maria."

"And Samuel. Debes beber menos."

"I told you already, I don't speak Spanish."

She smiled.

"I said you must drink less, I like you better when you are sober," she finished, turning around and heading at a fair pace back down the street. Samuel watched her go.

"And I liked you better without all that make-up," he whispered as she went.

~ ~ ~

Raul closed the door gently to his office. He'd grown bored of watching his dancing girls parading themselves about on stage to the same set of lost expressions week in, week out.

Relaxing into his most comfortable black, leather seat, he pressed the play button on his ageing VCR. Raul liked to think that he had many interests. The truth was they were all obsessions to varying degrees, more in control of him than he was of them. Part of him understood this, but still he chose to ignore those little voices who often tried to shed light on his abnormal condition. It was easier that way. Easier to turn a blind eye on reality when reality became too uncomfortable to bear. Hell, he'd been doing it all his adult life, so why should he stop now?

To stop and think about all those horrible things he'd seen as a child, or had gone on to do in the name of unhappiness and anger, was too terrible a thing to even contemplate. So Raul would do the next best thing. Raul liked to watch other people at play; other people who liked to do terrible things in the name of entertainment. In doing so he could always say, well at least I haven't done that! For a while this would make him feel better, but only for a short period. Soon, another fix would be required, and this one even stronger than the last.

The video began to play. Slowly, the images began to flash up on screen. Seeing them, he felt the first tingles of excitement and got himself more comfortable. Tonight he was in for a real treat. He hadn't seen this video before. It had come fresh from the rebel front line, sent to him from an old general friend who seemed to share the same unhealthy tastes as he did.

Raul was going to enjoy the video too, every last minute – or so he thought. He could hear the young girl's screams long before the captive rebel appeared on screen. Even then he didn't have a clear view, a handful of teenage soldiers having already formed a semi-circle in front of the camera. Raul sighed. After all the long hours of waiting, anticipating, he didn't want the evening to end in such disappointment, and only when the cameraman pushed forward could he begin to relax again. Raul was going to see everything this time.

"Boss?" a timid voice then sounded from outside his office.

Immediately, he switched off the VCR and for some minutes afterward, as Leopold continued to tap his knuckles against the door, he sat alone in his office, in near total darkness, deep in thought. He'd seen rape before, not through the use of modern technology, but first hand, as a boy when he'd still lived with his family back in Caquetá. Both his mother and sister had been raped by government soldiers. Their excuse? Rebel collaborators; which had been absurd, as no rebel soldier had ever stepped foot inside their quiet village.

The images from that day were still vivid, disturbing. Raul only had to close his eyes and they were there, in full colour, full audio. He didn't need a tape to replay them, and some nights he felt sure he would turn mad.

"Boss," Leopold again inquired, a little louder this time.

Quickly, Raul stood.

"Boss? You in there?"

"What is it Leo? You found me some business yet?" Raul replied, opening the door. Leopold shuffled back a few paces as his boss appeared.

"Well?"

Leopold knew he'd done a good job this time around. He'd stuck close to Samuel all night.

"He's in the square right now Raul, I came straight away to tell you."

"You sure?"

"Sure I'm sure."

"Then wait outside, I'll be with you soon," Raul finished, striding back into the office to retrieve his pistol and bullets which were scattered across his desk.

"Time to make us some money," he then mumbled to himself, loading the gun. In truth, money was all Raul cared about, and the power which money could buy. Perhaps enough power to protect your small family village the next time the bad men came calling.

~ ~ ~

Samuel had been asleep for no more than five minutes when he'd begun to dream of his father. He was still six in this particular dream, but he was no longer waiting outside his school gates for Jack Locke to pull up. Instead, he was stood outside the kitchen door of his old childhood home back in Bethnal Green, listening to his mother crying and her best friend doing what she could to console her. He'd stood outside that blasted door for nearly forty minutes, the first seeds of resentment towards his father slowly being sown. Jack had escaped prison several months previous and still there was no word from him.

"C'mon Samuel, time to go," a distant voice spoke. Gradually, Samuel opened his eyes. The earlier fireworks had long since died. The sky above was now a pitch black, and as he woke and sat upright, he found not Maria by his side, but instead the little, white haired old man he'd met in the salsa bar many hours previous, way before his clash with Maria. The old man was called Domingo. His body was short, wafer thin and mostly bent over through extreme age. Domingo had also been on his way to Santa Marta that evening and had showed Samuel where to wait as midnight approached. After leaving Maria, Samuel had made his way back to the main square, her strong words still ringing in his head. Maybe she was right. Perhaps he should just call it quits and go home.

"What is it?" Samuel now spoke, his head pounding something rotten from all the cheap beer he'd consumed.

"The bus, it's here," Domingo quickly replied, pointing a shaky finger toward a clapped out monster which now sat twenty yards or so in front of them; thick clouds of black smoke billowing from its rusted exhaust. As Samuel eyed the beast, its doors flew open, its tatty interior empty except for one bored looking driver. With some discomfort, Domingo pushed himself up from the bench.

"Last bus to Santa Marta Samuel. You come or stay?"

Samuel paused. The driver began to rev his engine.

"Well?" Domingo continued.

Samuel knew he couldn't leave. Not until he'd found his father.

"I'm staying," Samuel eventually replied, the fading memory of his dream having made up his mind.

"Then you must be careful young man..."

"I know, this town isn't safe for a chap like me," Samuel was quick to finish. Domingo smiled, and then very slowly, using a stick which looked almost as old as himself, he hobbled his way across the square and into the bus. Its doors soon closed, and both men found themselves waving one another farewell. Watching the bus wind its way out of town, Samuel climbed to his feet, the large amounts of beer he'd recently drunk making him feel queasy as he stood, and began to wander back across the square, heading for the ring of buildings that lined its borders.

He had no immediate plan other than to find a cheap hotel for the night, perhaps the next few nights depending on how well his enquiries went the following day. He'd find a half decent place and settle down for a good night's rest. His only real worry would be his lack of cash, having reconciled himself to the fact that by now both his back pack and camera would have been sold off by the hotel owner in Doncella.

He knew that he'd be in for a roasting if he were to call his editor back in London. But he also knew that underneath all the gruff John would wire him over emergency funds as and when the time came to beg hard enough. With this in mind, he reached the edge of the square. He was listening to the beat of distant salsa, its addictive tune making him want to sway, and was even beginning to consider a late night club when the sound of faint footsteps reached his ears.

Expecting to find a small group of revellers making their unsteady way home, perhaps on their way to a late night club themselves, Samuel glanced behind him. There were no revellers however.

Now having passed the same bench which he'd been using as a bed, a large group of Colombian males came to a halt. Samuel counted eight of them. They were tall, broad men, each grasping a knife and with pieces of cloth wrapped about their faces. In his intoxicated state, Samuel could not help thinking of the Lone Ranger and began to chuckle. Despite this, his instincts were still sharp enough for him to realize that he was now in great danger. These men were obviously out to rob him, perhaps even worse. He'd most likely been spotted drinking alone in the salsa bar and now their entire flock had gathered to pick over his remains.

"Ola! How are you?" he yelled, even raising an arm to wave at them.

A little bewildered by the Westerner's sudden show of bravado, the bandits glanced at one another. Samuel had managed to down several whiskeys that evening. Usually this turned him violent, but tonight it only made him reckless. He didn't want them to think that he was afraid, which of course he was.

One by one the Colombians started forward. At first Samuel turned casually away and began walking toward the buildings before him. His eyes then fixed on the nearest alleyway and he burst into a sprint. The Colombians, half expecting this, had already begun to jog. Now seeing him make a break for it, they too broke into a sprint. There would be no point in trying to reason with them. Samuel was not that drunk. He knew the score well enough. Strangers like him went missing in Colombia almost every day. Indeed, it had become almost routine. The police didn't seem to care either, they were pretty much corrupt themselves, and a large gang of opportunist thieves like the ones which now hurtled after him, wouldn't think twice about slicing open his throat for a few paltry dollars.

Nearly out of breath, Samuel turned a sharp corner and came face to face with a high brick wall. Already he could hear the rapid tread of heavy footsteps approaching him and in a matter of seconds he knew their owners would be beating him to a pulp. He glanced at a shaky looking trellis that clung to the wall and made a desperate leap for it, the first of many men beginning to emerge from the shadows as he did. Luckily, he managed to grab a firm hold of the trellis's bottom rung and quickly began to haul himself up.

After a long struggle, he reached the final rung of the trellis and managed to throw his weary body onto the adjacent rooftop. Far down below, the Colombians had begun to climb the wall also, not quite ready yet to let their prey go. Seeing them, Samuel fell to his knees, and using all his remaining strength, tried to snap the trellis free. No luck. Each time he tried his fingertips only turned numb from the intense effort and the Colombians were now only inches from reaching him.

Again he panicked, he bolted across the rooftop, often having to skip from one building to the next, praying he wouldn't slip and fall into one of the many narrow streets which riddled the town some distance below. Occasionally, the odd firework would explode overhead, briefly shedding his haphazard pathway in light. This was all very well until there sounded a particularly loud explosion that caused Samuel to lose his footing, sending him careering through an open skylight.

It had taken Samuel only a second to disappear from view, amidst a hail of twirling splinters and glass, and as the Colombians reached the rooftop soon after, they were mystified at such a peculiar vanishing act. It took them several minutes of hard head scratching before the brightest amongst them figured out what had happened. By this time Samuel was already on his feet, if a little dazed, and planning his escape all over again.

~ ~ ~

"I hope you can forgive me Jack," Shelley mumbled to himself as he climbed the steps to the mayoral office. Outside its door he lit a cigarette and listened to the sounds of growing panic emanating from within. It was all perfectly understandable. A month previous the rebels had issued a series of threats: All town mayors, those of whom were loyal to the government, were to abandon their posts or face immediate execution. At first none of those in power had listened. The rebels often made outlandish declarations such as these, but very rarely acted on them.

Their main job was to create fear and whatever disruption this fear could wreak upon Colombia's already less than solid infrastructure. None of the mayors had reckoned on them going through with their chilling plan of controlled, sustained slaughter, and only when the first mayor, from a small town far to the south, had been found decapitated in his bathroom, did the others take note and begin to question their immediate futures.

"You busy?"

Sevilla's mayor was moving fast for a man pushing seventy and only allowed himself a peek at Shelley as the Englishman stepped into his practically empty office.

"What you want? I no talk now!" Greco snapped. He looked worn out, large beads of sweat running down either side of his thin face.

"I could give you a hand; you have a lot of boxes that need shifting."

"I be okay on my own!"

Shelley leaned against the door frame. The town appeared to be so peaceful that evening. He looked to the twinkling of houselights in the far distance and then, for a time, as Greco continued to pack, he watched a collection of moths hover about the room's single light bulb. It was as if there were no such people as the rebels. Their kind simply couldn't exist, not when everything was so tranquil.

Shelley didn't want to run out on Jack, but he felt that Jack had forced him into this very difficult position. It was something he'd thought long and hard about and in the end it seemed to be the only option left available to him. In a lot of ways he blamed himself. He'd known Jack for almost forty years and had come to understand how stubborn a man he could be once an idea had taken root. The trouble was however that some of his ideas could turn out to be bloody awful ones and there had been numerous occasions where Shelley had needed to bail his old friend out of trouble.

It would not be possible, Shelley was convinced, to recall all the bar brawls, shootouts and other scrapes which had taken place whenever one of Jack's terrific ideas had gone pear-shaped. Too many to mention; and yet during all those years Shelley had somehow managed to stick by him, even when it would have been easier to just up sticks and go their separate ways. Shelley was getting older, so was

Jack and what had constituted fun and adventure in their younger days had become tiresome and often fearful in their twilight years. At least for Shelley. In his honest opinion, Jack would never grow up. Not properly. He would remain the largest fourteen year old even if he were to reach one hundred and neither Shelley nor anybody else could ever change that fact. Jack was a one off.

The man had so many merits, and yet so many faults; you never quite knew where you stood with him: Cantankerous; arrogant and reckless – yes; but also charming, forgiving, brave and above all – his friend.

"You still 'ere?" Greco continued, stuffing a bundle of papers into the nearest box. All the boxes were now full and the papers only just fitted after a great deal of shoving.

"You leave tomorrow?" Shelley asked mournfully.

"Si, si, tomorrow."

"I'd like to come with you; I'd be safer with you and your men."

"No! No! No! No!"

"I have cash, not much, but you can have it all."

Greco paused, his wrinkled hands clutching other papers and various bits and pieces. Slowly, he looked toward Shelley, right into Shelley's eyes.

"If I get caught with you...They cut my throat!" he replied, dropping what was left of the papers to the floor, realizing there was no more room to be had in any of the surrounding boxes.

"What about your friend, eh? What about Jack?" he continued.

"What about Jack?"

"You go together no? Better chance together I think."

"I'm afraid Jack feels happier where he is," Shelley replied, having said the same thing to his friend on many occasions.

"Then he is loco...A crazy man!"

Greco was right about that too. Jack was crazy, both crazy and greedy which was a very dangerous combination, especially when stuck in the middle of Colombia.

"Then you must talk to him. If the rebels come, they kill you both!" Greco continued, trying to close one of the box lids. The contents of the box were having none of it and bravely refused all attempts at being shut in.

"You need a hand there?"

"I okay, you worry about yourself."

"I think Jack is a little crazy, but what can I do?"

"Convince him, you must!"

"Convince Jack, you make it sound so very simple Greco, I'm not surprised they elected you mayor."

Shelley took another long drag on his cigarette. Talking to Jack was no longer an option. Jack wouldn't listen to him. In his mind Sevilla was safe from any imminent rebel attack. The ransom money was on its way so what would be the point in leaving? Only a coward would run at the first hint of trouble, and Jack Locke was no coward. He'd sooner die in battle than have the yellow tag pinned on him.

"They here any day now Shelley... Any day!" Greco went on, having admitted defeat with the box and now taking a well-earned rest across its top. Even with his weight pressing down against the flimsy cardboard, the flaps were still unable to close properly. Shelley thought he resembled some kind of obscene Jack-in-the-box, ready to be launched high into the air, as and when the box's contents exploded.

Shelley left the door frame and strolled over to where Greco sat. He took a seat next to the old mayor and this time the box was forced closed.

"Cigarette?"

"Gracias."

Greco took the cigarette from Shelley's hand and slipped it into the corner of his mouth.

"Jack thinks the rebels are all bluff, he doesn't think they'll come at all to Sevilla."

"I told you, Jack is loco," Greco replied, speaking through the free corner of his mouth as Shelley lit the cigarette.

"Loco, loco, loco!"

"We're expecting the first of our ransom money tomorrow afternoon. The silly bugger wants to stay and wait for the other families to pay up!" Shelley continued.

Through the thin cloud of smoke which would soon clog the entire office Greco smiled.

"I know nothing of kidnapping or any wrongdoing in this town friend."

"Of course not Greco, your hands are clean."

"Almost as clean as yours, I think."

Shelley grinned. Colombia really was a great country. Anyone could be bought.

"He plans on staying another month."

Greco shook his head.

"I hear rumours in town Shelley; they say the rebels will be here within the week."

"They may just turn out to be rumours."

Greco shrugged.

"Perhaps, but I will not wait here to find out."

Both men fell silent. Jack had allowed money to blind his better judgment – the stupid, greedy bastard.

"You can leave with us tomorrow if you like Shelley, but you must be ready."

"Are you sure?"

"No, but I feel sorry for you. Any friend of Jack and I feel sorry for him."

Shelley stood. Greco also rose. He looked like he was in some kind of pain too, a hand moving quickly to his back.

"Can I think about it? Jack is a good pal after all."

"We leave tomorrow afternoon, you have until then," Greco finished, turning away from Shelley to see if there was anything else he could take from the room. The room was practically bare.

"Until then," Shelley replied, leaving the office.

6

Kidnapped

"Don't you ever listen to me?"

Samuel squirmed about the stage in pain. This had to be a dream. He began to blink; a flurry of blinks followed, but still the peculiar image remained. Maria was standing half naked over him, a large python writhing about her upper torso.

He wanted to sit up but the nagging pain he felt in his lower back told him to lie still for a moment and try to regain what bearings he had left. This had to be some kind of dream.

"Are you hurt badly?" Maria continued, kneeling down next to him. The python was beginning to wrap itself about her neck. She quickly, expertly uncoiled the beast and set it gently down onto the stage. Other curious lap dancing girls had now arrived to gawk at their strange new arrival. Samuel glared up at them as

Chris Sanders

Maria helped him to lean against one of the many silver poles cramming the stage. Above the girls he could see a host of bright, flashing lights and beyond these, as his senses returned, the open skylight through which he'd so recently fallen.

"Samuel, say something," Maria again spoke. Her voice was soft, and Samuel nearly missed her soothing tone on account of the loud music being pumped from every corner of the strip club.

"Samuel?"

"I'm okay."

"You sure?"

Slowly, Samuel began to twist his neck and back; a few creaks but nothing major.

"I hurt like hell but I don't think anything's broken," he replied.

"Can you walk?"

"If you give me a second."

"I'd like to give you a slap, following me was stupid!"

"I wasn't following you, I..."

"And please Samuel, don't start your lies again."

Samuel bit his tongue, allowing Maria and a few of the other girls to help him off stage. He moved slowly at first, still feeling quite dizzy from his fall. By this time the python had slithered off, attracted to the group of confused men who crammed perverts row. Was this all part of the act? Seeing the snake approach, they began to scatter.

"I'm surprised you are not dead after that," Maria continued, holding Samuel steady as they made their way through the seedy strip joint. Passing one of the club's tables he reached over and stole a glass of beer.

"I was being chased," he spoke between long gulps.

"Chased? By who?"

"Didn't stop to ask them Maria," he continued, both of them having reached the club's entrance.

"You know, you can't stay here right?" Maria spoke, her eyes constantly darting back toward Raul's office. Any second now he'd step out. She was sure.

"But I got no other place to go Maria!"

"Then you should have taken your bus!"

They both paused, Maria's thoughts working overtime.

"Here, take this," she went on, pulling out a key from the tiny pouch which looped its way around her waist.

"What's this for?"

"For my flat, I see you there later, okay?"

"But what about your boyfriend?"

She threw a nervous glance again toward the office.

"Look, there is no boyfriend; I live alone, now please you have to go!"

"But I..."

Even as he spoke the door to the office began to open. Seeing this, Maria panicked, first kicking the entrance door wide and then pushing Samuel out into the street.

"Later Samuel!" she said, slamming the door in his face.

"But I can't remember where you live," he murmured softly into the door. He was thinking of giving the chunk of wood a hard boot himself when a small stone suddenly hit the back of his head.

"Christ!" he yelled, spinning around to find the same group of Colombians who'd chased him onto the roof top now standing a few short paces in front,, their funny little masks still in place.

"Look guys, I don't have much cash," Samuel said, watching as the group of men began to form a semi-circle about him. The tallest of the eight was stepping forward when Samuel made a calculated dash for the door. He only got as far as its handle, however, when something a lot harder than a stone met the back of his head, and again he was sent to sleep.

~ ~ ~

Joseph Robinson Walker Jnr stuffed the last piece of stale bread into his hungry mouth and washed it down with what little amount of dirtied water remained in his tiny bowl. He then belched. It tasted good, real good. Not as good as a quarter pounder with fries would taste, but good enough after going without food for five painfully long hours. Joseph was not used to waiting, for anything. Money had always come easy to Joseph.

His parents were both wealthy and pushovers: Fast cars and the finest clothes had never been out of reach. Neither had drugs. He loved cocaine; he'd once heard somebody say that when you could afford to snort coke every day you were earning too much cash. Perhaps that was true, except that Joseph had never earned a dime in his young life. To Joseph money was something you simply asked for and then got given. And once you had the money, why then you could start having fun, real fun. Joseph would be twenty next fall.

It had come as quite a shock then when, one early summer morning, Joseph Robinson Walker Snr had stopped by the family swimming pool to talk to his only son who'd been sunbathing for the past hour. Walker Snr had been meaning to talk with his son for some time, and only when their most recent phone bill had arrived, once again extortionate, had he finally decided that enough was enough. That morning Walker Snr had told his son in no uncertain terms that unless he got off his lazy ass and did something constructive with his life there would be no more easy cash to spend. At first Joseph had taken the news quite calmly. Why not? Threats such as these had been levelled before, indeed many times before, and he'd always managed to charm, or nag his parents into changing their minds. Have faith he'd tell them. Your son knows exactly what he's doing.

That much was true. For the past year he'd been having a damn good time. College was a distant, unhealthy rumour and all at his parents' great expense. But the cold, determined look which he'd found in his father's eyes that bright, sunny morning had sent a cold chill right through Joseph's flabby, overweight body. This time his father had meant what he'd said and the following days were to bear his words out.

Joseph was soon to discover that all his credit cards had been cut up; his new car taken away, and as for the escort services – well, the receptionist would hang up just as soon as they recognized his voice. In effect, young Joe's wild life of excess had come to a sudden, juddering halt.

Joseph happily necked the last drops of water from his bowl before stealing a glance across his cell to where the newcomer had been dropped early last night. He hadn't appeared to of moved since then and now young Joe was starting to worry.

"Hey pal, are you okay over there?" he asked, waiting patiently for a response. None came.

"Leave the poor kid alone, he's probably still in shock," a stern voice answered from somewhere inside the cell. The surrounding shadows hid its owner. Joseph thought it was Mike but he couldn't be sure. For three weeks he'd been locked up with Mike and David. During that difficult period none of them had been given a great deal to drink, and even less to eat. Consequently, they were all very weak.

Their voices had begun to crackle under this constant strain and so now it had become difficult to distinguish one voice properly from the next.

"Hey, pal, you okay?" Joseph went on, this time picking up his bowl and throwing it toward Samuel. He hit his target.

"Wakey, wakey sleepy!"

Samuel slowly removed the dirty pile of rags which had been thrown over him and began to force his bleary eyes wide. He hadn't been drugged this time around. Although the back of his head ached something terrible, it was still clear. He could still think.

"Where the hell am I?" he mumbled. He could see that he was propped against the far wall of a long, narrow corridor. A small amount of light filtered down into this space via a single barred window which began near the ceiling and came to an end only a few inches down. He wasn't alone either. There were others with him. Other shapes at least. He couldn't see faces clearly, only bodies under rags like him.

"First question they always ask...Good question too. Still, I don't always tell them. Best that way...What's your name anyway friend?" the voice continued.

Its owner sat opposite him. A fat kid with dark blond hair and a patchy blond moustache beneath a stubby nose.

"You have a name friend?" Joseph went on.

"I told you Joe, leave the poor kid alone, he needs his rest," Mike muttered from beneath his sheets at the other end of the cell.

"Ah, go back to sleep Mike, nobody wants to hear what you have to say," Joseph replied.

"So what's your name?" he persisted, facing Samuel once again.

"Samuel, stupid Samuel."

"Well good to meet you stupid, my name's Joseph, but you can call me Joe."

"And where the hell am I, Joe?"

"Don't tell him," Mike chipped in.

"He don't wanna know!"

"You're in deep shit Samuel, but not to worry, you look like a real nice guy, I'm sure your parents will have you out of here in no time, no time at all."

"Don't listen to him kid, he's been here for over three months now and nobody's even tried to rescue his ass!" Mike went on, even louder than before.

"Ignore him Sammy, he just likes to talk crap. Believe me my folks are on the case right now. Any day and I'm out of here. I mean I know I screwed up. I had one last chance. Pops gave me cash to go to college, but I thought nah, to hell with it, I'll go to South America instead! I know I screwed up!"

Samuel didn't reply. He didn't want a chat with Joseph. The guy obviously had a screw loose. He didn't want to be here at all.

"So, where you from Sammy? You sound sorta English to me."

"London, I'm from London."

"London! No shit, I'm from New York, Manhattan, ever been to New York Sammy?"

Samuel was about to reply when a huge trap door opened up overhead. A flood of bright light spilled into the cell and for the first time Samuel could see a long, wooden ladder running up toward the roof.

"Christ! We got company Sammy. Now do what I say, act like you're asleep, sometimes they like to beat us for fun!" Joseph began to whisper.

"It's just you who they like to beat!" Mike spoke up as two pairs of feet began to descend the steps. As they did, Samuel could hear the sound of many sheets being pulled over heads. Feeling suddenly uneasy, he did the same. He curled himself into a tight ball and then listened as the footsteps approached gradually. Quite soon, they had reached the position where he lay. He braced himself, expecting a boot at any moment.

"This one, it's this one boss," somebody, who stood rather too close, spoke.

"This one? You sure it's him?" a familiar voice replied.

Tentatively, Samuel pulled back his covers.

"Oh, Jesus! It is you!" Shelley proclaimed, genuinely surprised with their new hostage.

"Is that any sort of welcome?" Samuel replied, sitting himself upright once more. Directly behind Shelley stood the skinny Colombian kid who owned the itchy trigger finger.

"I thought we'd told you to clear off, Mr. Locke?"

"You did, but I don't always do what I'm told."

"So we've noticed. Well, you're in a lot of trouble this time around, young man. A great deal of trouble. And to think my poor men thought they'd bagged someone of real worth. How disappointing life can be at times. We should have plastered your picture to the walls and told them to keep well clear!"

"Does this mean I get to meet my father now Shelley?"

Shelley sighed.

"Untie him Saul."

"But boss!"

"I said bloody untie him didn't I?" Shelley snapped.

Reluctantly, Saul knelt beside Samuel and began to untie both his arms and legs.

"You know, I thought those guys were going to kill me last night Shelley. If I'd known they worked for you I would have made it a lot easier," Samuel joked as Saul battled with his knots. The knots were complicated and would take time to unravel.

"You should concern yourself with your own welfare, Mr. Locke. Our men can take care of themselves," Shelley replied.

"Please, call me Samuel."

Eventually, the knots were untied and Samuel was allowed to stand. All three men were heading for the ladder when Joseph threw off his rags and began to yell.

"Hey! What the hell about me? When do I get to leave?"

"Your turn will come Mr. Walker, have patience, I'm sure your parents won't leave you here to rot," Shelley was quick to reply, his foot already on the first rung of the ladder, both Samuel and Saul on his heels.

"Yeah, well screw you! Screw you too Sammy boy, I knew you were one of them. From the very start I knew it!"

"Put a plug in it Joe," either Dave or Mike mumbled from somewhere inside the cell.

"I knew it all along!" Joseph finished regardless, watching the last of the three men climb back through the trap door. Not long after, the door was lowered gently into place, and once again the hostages were pitched into darkness.

The cell trap door had been closed and locked. Samuel was standing in a wide courtyard, Shelley and Saul on either flank. He was still in Sevilla.

The same lush, green mountains rose high above the courtyard's turreted walls.

"Nice place you have here," Samuel quipped, studying the dozen or so armed guards who were dotted between these turrets, one or two of them even looking back and pointing their rifles at him. Shelley, who was already several paces up ahead replied: "Follow me please, less chatter; you wish to meet with somebody, remember?"

To underline his point, Saul gave Samuel a sharp nudge in the back with the business end of his rifle. Together, they walked past a large bonfire which had been built next to the courtyard's entrance, the entrance itself being a large, wooden gate. Samuel, who'd now caught up with Shelley commented:

"Another party?"

"Something like that."

They were headed for a tall building which stood at the far end of the courtyard. Other, similar buildings ringed the courtyard, each one boasting a single door and shuttered window. Samuel noticed a small, wooden cross had been nailed above the door of the building they now made for, and on either side two empty alcoves were present where he supposed statues had once sat.

"This place used to be a nunnery you know...El Convento del Santo Ecce Homo," Shelley declared, having picked up on Samuel's interest.

"But the nuns were chased away years ago," he continued. He took frantic little steps as he spoke and Samuel found himself thinking of Chaplin.

"Are you a religious man Samuel?"

"No not really, I've never been one for mass hysteria."

"Well, you've come to the right place then. Your pops will be thrilled."

Samuel now noticed large pieces of broken crockery littering the courtyard as they approached the building and was about to point this out when a loud shot rang out. He flinched, and then froze. Both Shelley and Saul stopped and glanced back at him, Saul's long wavy hair briefly masking his dark features as he turned.

"Do hurry up Samuel...Isn't polite to keep somebody waiting."

"But that gunshot."

"Nothing to worry about, just your father doing a spot of target practice, that's all."

"Target practice?"

A second later, a second gunshot rang out. Again, Samuel flinched.

"And who's the bloody target?" he barked as several pieces of pottery began to fall from the air and land maybe an inch or two from his right leg.

Shelley and Saul continued to walk, ignoring him.

"Shelley!" Samuel yelled, jogging after them.

"I asked you a question Shelley!" he continued having caught them up. A third gunshot exploded high overhead. This time all three men stopped as two complete plates came crashing down to earth less than a foot before them.

"Quite a shame, damn fine crockery too. Ran clean out of chickens a week ago," Shelley observed, stepping casually over what remained of the plates, his focus back on the building ahead.

"Move it!" Saul snapped, again digging the rifle into Samuel's ribs, this time with an extra bit of force.

They entered the ex-convent through a veil of multi-coloured, hanging beads. A tall, spiral staircase then led them onto the rooftop. Samuel's stomach began to flutter with many different kinds of butterfly. His throat felt suddenly dry too. He'd been waiting for this moment all his life and now that it was here he could feel himself slowly seizing up, like an engine almost out of fuel. He was afraid, even a little bit excited. He tried to make himself angry as he climbed the spiral staircase but it was hopeless. Instead, he felt like a naughty schoolboy again who was about to get the rollicking of his life. He felt around six years old.

~ ~ ~

Jack Locke bellowed:
"Throw another one Mario!"
"And this time throw it bloody right!" he continued, raising the impressive looking shotgun to his shoulder.

A mound of plates sat to his left. A young boy, no older than fourteen, stood next to this pile.

"Fire when ready Mario!"

Mario hurled one of the plates high into the air. Jack fired, Jack missed.

"You're not throwing them properly Mario! Can't you do anything right?"

The boy stood still, silent. Jack began to re-load the shotgun, his broad back still turned on Shelley and his companions.

"You still with us Samuel?" Shelley asked, having noted Samuel's pallid complexion.

"Samuel?"

"I don't think I can do this, Shelley."

"A little late in the day for that kind of talk don't you think?"

"Quite probably... But all the same I'd rather not be here."

Samuel could not take his eyes off Jack as he spoke to Shelley. Almost twenty years had flown by but Samuel still found he recognized the tall, lean figure that belonged to his father. The blonde locks had long since gone and now a fine mop of silvery hair grew untidily from the top of his head.

"Come along Samuel," Shelley nagged, slowly beginning to walk toward Jack and the boy. Cautiously, Samuel followed.

"Again!" Jack yelled.

A second plate was hurled into the clear blue sky. Jack fired and this time scored. He jumped with glee as he watched the plate explode into a thousand tiny pieces.

"What do you say to that one Mario then? A crack shot or what?"

"I think you got lucky," came the boy's droll reply.

Shelley waited for his friend's euphoria to die down. When it had he coughed quietly into his hand.

"Is he with you Shelley?" Jack asked without turning around, replacing the shotgun's empty barrel with two new cartridges.

"Yes Jack, Samuel's here."

"Then tell him to stand next to me will you."

Samuel glanced nervously toward Shelley. Shelley gave him a brief nod and then took a step back. They were similar, Shelley thought, perhaps not in character but certainly in build. Samuel had Jack's keen blue eyes and both men walked with the same laid back, easy gait.

"I didn't believe Shelley when he told me it was you...I suppose you can't blame me for that one?" Jack spoke. Samuel kept his council, content at first to just watch his father.

"Take hold of this, Samuel."

Jack passed the shotgun carefully to his son.

"Be gentle with her Samuel, she's my favourite toy," he spoke, facing Samuel for the first time.

Jack Locke had turned sixty a few months previous, but looked a good five years younger. Although he smoked only a few packets of cigarettes a week, these being a particularly light brand, he drank like an absolute witch and only ever slept a few hours each night. It was a miracle he looked so good.

Jack had led a wild life. From his early years as a gangster in London's East End to the present day, he'd always embraced excess. He'd had little formal education and yet found it easy to talk his way into any social group; invariably dominating it through sheer strength of personality and a handsome, commanding presence. A man amongst men, Jack Locke considered himself rightly above the law and had led his life in strict accordance with this thinking. Nobody could touch him, would ever touch him. He would surprise you. He'd even surprise himself.

"Now hold her steady, and remember Samuel..."

"I know, squeeze the trigger slowly," Samuel interrupted, preparing to fire.

"Good lad, you turned out half decent."

"No thanks to you."

"Fire!" Jack boomed. Mario released another plate high into the clear Colombian air. For a split second, Samuel tracked its flight and then pulled the trigger. He missed. The plate fell to earth.

"You lived with your mother for too long, that's your problem boy."

"Don't mention my mother Jack...She's worth a thousand of you!"

"You came all this way just to criticize?"

"Don't flatter yourself."

"Then we'll call it chance!"

"Call it whatever you like."

Jack smiled, taking the gun away from his son and then handing it to Mario.

"Put her away Mario,"

Mario scuttled off. Jack took a seat at one of the dozen tables which sat across the rooftop and motioned for Samuel to do the same. After a moment's hesitation, he obliged. Shelley and Saul had retreated downstairs some time ago. Samuel gazed thoughtfully out over the courtyard. The late afternoon light had begun to fade. Down below, the bonfire had been lit. Large men with bull whips stood around this fire, cracking their whips as the blaze built.

"They believe it keeps away evil spirits...Bloody fools!" Jack remarked, turning from the fire to watch Mario return, a vintage bottle of champagne in one hand, two glasses in the other.

"Drink?"

"I could do with one."

"Good fellow. I never could trust a man who didn't like a drink now and then. Isn't natural."

Mario poured them each a glass of champagne and then, as if following a prior order, he left the rooftop.

"Shelley told me all about your little game," Samuel began.

"Well, Shelley has a big mouth."

"Still, I'd like to hear it from you, the truth that is, none of your bullshit!"

"La verdad es una puta y hay que pagar!"

"I'm sorry Pops but I don't speak the lingo."

"Disappointing; to think of all those fine schools I sent you to."

"Jack..."

"I said truth is a whore and you must pay for her."

"Well I'm afraid I'm broke at the moment, would you accept a cheque?"

"Never! I run a strict cash only operation."

Samuel took a sip from his glass. He still felt intimidated by his father and needed to loosen up.

"How is your mother by the way?"

"Sooner die than mention your name."

Jack grinned.

"Yes quite, I suppose I can't blame the old girl either."

"You wouldn't dare, not even you could be that arrogant," Samuel replied. Jack ignored this last comment and very nearly necked the glass of champagne. After some time had passed he spoke:

"I'm in a spot of trouble here Samuel; I expect Shelley told you this too?"

"Briefly."

"We're running short on cash you see. At the moment we're waiting on ransom money, but the people involved have been dragging their feet somewhat. Families don't appear to be as close these days."

"So I've noticed."

"Still, I'm sure everything will come good at the last minute."

"Couldn't you just slip away? You're good at that."

"I wish I could, I really do, but take a good look around. Each one of my men carries a gun, and all of them want paying. Besides I couldn't just abandon the hostages. Most of them are just kids. I could never be that cold. Wouldn't be right. So you see we're practically prisoners here until we get our hands on some cash."

"I'm sure you'll think of something."

The crowd surrounding the bonfire was beginning to grow.

"Colombians love their parties, don't they Samuel?"

"Don't go changing the subject."

"I believe it's some sort of local ceremony. A voodoo thing. Couldn't picture it in Bethnal Green though."

"All still a big game to you isn't it Jack?"

"That's right son, and at the moment the stakes are pretty high."

"I waited for you to get in touch. All those years and not even a God damn letter! Pretty stupid of me really."

"It was better that way."

"Better for you maybe...I was too young to understand."

Jack had stopped listening. His eyes were back on the courtyard, watching the bonfire build as the surrounding crowds continued to hurl pieces of wood and loose rubbish into its heart.

Music could be heard. Through the flames, Jack glimpsed a traditional Vallenato band: accordion, drums, guaracharaca, scrapper, bass guitar and trumpet. He would have to leave these people soon and it wouldn't be easy. He was still looking into the bonfire, through the bonfire, when he spoke:

"I have a grave responsibility to these people Samuel, I've drawn them all into a dangerous situation and now I have to stay and come good on my promises."

"I never knew you had a conscience," Samuel sniped.

"I came here five years ago. Colombians don't speak much English, but I helped set up a small school and started to teach the kids. I was doing something good for once. Something of worth. The kids went home and taught their families, but you know what Samuel, you can't escape your nature, not really. Jesus, you can try, but it will always find you, wherever you run too...These people put their trust in me, and I can't let them down."

"You once had a wife and son back home."

"I told you already...It was better I stayed away...Better for everybody concerned."

As he spoke, a trickle of people spilled onto the rooftop. They carried with them large bottles of strong Columbiana and all looked much the worse for drink.

"I think they want us to join in their party."

"You go on; I'm not in the right frame of mind."

"Nonsense! No son of Jack Locke will be a wet blanket. That's one of the unofficial rules, on your feet boy!" Jack ordered, already standing, grasping the half drunk bottle of champagne.

"Never turn down a good invitation either, that's another rule Samuel, you never know where it might lead to."

"Do I have any say in this?"

"None whatsoever. Now, on your feet."

Grabbing Samuel's hand, Jack hauled his son clean off the chair. A band of merry locals soon enveloped them.

"I still have a lot of questions Dad."

"Well you can ask me all the questions you want tomorrow, right before you leave."

"Leave?"

"I've arranged for a bus to collect you tomorrow afternoon, I'll give you some cash and then you can be on your way."

"And what if I say no?"

"Then you'd be a bloody fool!" Jack laughed. The locals began to laugh. Together, arms slung around one another's shoulders, they made their way down into the courtyard.

7

Rose Tinted Glasses

Maria sat on the very edge of her bed. She was looking at the tiny replica house which she'd built together with her mother not long before her fifth Christmas. The Pesebre evoked both good and bad memories for her. The idea behind the model was to make a replica of a town where everyone welcomes Jesus. It was done every Christmas and was usually finished by the sixteenth. How elaborate it became depended on how strong your imagination was, how powerful your capacity for dreaming could be. That particular year a lot of work had gone into their Pesebre. She could still see her mother's nimble fingers hard at work on the creation: Pebbles, sticks, dried grass and a variety of flowers had all been used to build the house. They'd even used light, blue paper to make the sky and then littered it with a field of silvery stars.

Over the years, Maria had taken good care of the house. It had been the last house mother and daughter had built together, and after all that time, it still looked as good as new. It was a shame she could not say that about her real town. Good memories, bad memories. Maria looked absently out her bedroom window. That same Christmas the rebels had arrived and laid siege on Sevilla. The police station had been attacked first, its officers easily outnumbered. It looked as though the rebels would go on a terrible rampage through the town, killing and pillaging as they went, snatching young teenagers from their families and turning them into the next generation of soldiers.

But to their credit the town's civilians had stood up and said no. Enough was enough. They'd lived in fear for far too long, and now that the threat had become real, was on their very doorstep, action was going to be taken. Although only five at the time, Maria could still recall Sevilla's faithful locals, both young and old, rushing to the defence of their beloved town. She could still hear the gunshots ring out and picture the town square ablaze in the aftermath of battle.

Mother had been on her way to see her cousins. She'd been crossing the square when the rebels had first attacked. They'd shot her dead in the ensuing crossfire. Another civilian casualty. One of thousands in Colombia. Fifteen years had passed and yet nothing had improved. Not for

Maria, not for Sevilla. Its people were again beginning to fear the very worst; rumours being widespread of a further rebel attack.

Sevilla's mayor, the damn coward, was already preparing to flee and without any backup from the government military, Sevilla was nothing more than a sitting duck again.

Maria began to change for work. Samuel had not been waiting for her at the flat as she'd expected. At first she'd been cross, but now, almost twenty four hours later, she could only feel concern. She liked Samuel and felt genuinely attracted to him: his quiet, complex nature, the self-confident manner in which he carried himself; the vulnerability which undoubtedly bubbled away beneath. Those clear, blue eyes of his. You could swim in those eyes of his, she thought, zipping up her black, leather boots. She could only hope that he was okay, that he'd come to no harm. Certainly there was nothing she could do. Raul had a lot of influence in town but telling him would only condemn the boy even further.

With or without Samuel, one day, she promised herself on her late mother's grave, one day she would make it out of Sevilla for good. She left the flat having put Samuel clean out of her mind, her thoughts once more focused on work. Like every other night she would have to dance well into the early hours. She made little cash for her efforts and Raul would take most of it for himself. Once her shift was over she'd stumble back to the flat. She'd sleep until the following afternoon and then wake only to start the same routine over again. Nothing changed. Not for a girl like Maria. Not in Sevilla.

By six thirty in the morning the bonfire had burnt itself out, as had the party. Sleeping revellers and their bottles lay strewn across the courtyard. Only one amongst them had had the energy to stay awake. Jack Locke lit his fourth cigarette that morning, staring into the blackened mess at his feet, watching the last funnels of smoke gently rise from its ashes.

He could see a lot of Rachael in Samuel. He could see more of himself in Samuel too, than in any of his other six children that were scattered about the globe. Still, Sam was special in one more important respect. Samuel had been his first born, his rightful heir to whatever fortune he might one day of chanced upon, and so deserved his fair share of meditation. Soul searching was not completely alien to Jack. As the years passed he would find himself thinking more seriously about certain matters, whereas before, during his younger, carefree days, he would have simply confined any worries to the back of his mind and cracked on with life. It had always been the best solution.

He loved Samuel. He'd always love Samuel. He'd spent six years with the child and had very nearly walked down the aisle with his mother; a beautiful lass he often recalled. The other offspring he'd only ever heard about, usually having skipped town long before any pregnancy had come to his attention. Samuel was different then. He'd got to know the lad, if only for a brief period of time; quite a sensitive soul too if he remembered correctly. Another trait he would have inherited from his dear mother. And so what now? What else could he do except send the boy away and make sure he was safe. That was the most responsible thing to do wasn't it? And God knows he had a lot of catching up to do in that department.

He flicked his cigarette into the fire and then watched it slowly disintegrate. He'd often stood and watched from a distance young families at play together. He'd often thought how happy they looked and how lucky they were to have one another. A black sheet would then tumble across his emotions whenever these thoughts popped into his head and he'd have to reassure himself that every hard decision that he'd ever taken had been for the best.

Stay in London. Go straight and set up home. Nonsense! Jack was no fool. He understood his maverick nature well enough by now to know that following that particular route would have been a complete disaster. He was no family man. He had love to give, but he could never be happy tied down to one street, one house, one family. Never. He would die alone and that was fine.

Rachael and Samuel had been better off without him. If he'd stayed he would have brought them nothing but trouble. So whenever the pain of 'what if' reared its ugly head he would refer his brain to these earlier thoughts and have done with it. Time to crack on with life.

"Jack?" Jack turned to find Shelley walking toward him.

"Are you okay there? You look deep in thought."

"Do you remember the Cock and Crow back in Bethnal Green?"

"Our first pub...Of course I remember it."

"We used to store all our stolen goods down below in the cellar didn't we? Tonnes of the stuff."

"I know. You made me shift most of it. My poor back still gives me gyp!"

"There was always a fight on for that pub wasn't there? Different gangs, wide boys, bent coppers. We never had a moment's peace."

"And?"

"And we enjoyed it, we enjoyed the brawls, the danger didn't we? It made life exciting, especially as we always seemed to come out on top."

"A long time ago Jack, I can't remember everything, what was your point again?"

"The point is Shelley that Rachael and Samuel were better off without me. I mean I was nothing more than just a troublemaker."

"I wouldn't go that far, we made some pretty decent cash."

"But leaving like that, I did the right thing didn't I?"

Shelley turned his head slowly toward the fire. He knew what Jack wanted to hear, and he knew how uncomfortable the truth would be to him.

"That girl loved you Jack, a word from you and she would have moved anywhere."

"Well thank you Shelley, next time I'll ask somebody else."

Shelley grinned.

"Given any more thought to leaving?" he continued, his face growing tense even as he'd posed the question. The topic of leaving town had become a huge sticking point between both men over the last few days and he knew that bringing the subject up again would only cause further disagreement.

"No," came the brisk reply.

"But the rebels could be here any day now Jack. Perhaps even tomorrow if the local gossip is to be believed."

Jack kept his eyes on what remained of the fire. He wasn't going to be drawn on the subject of leaving town. In his mind Sevilla was safe from any rebel attack and Shelley's attitude surprised him. After all the adventures they'd shared together down the years he wanted to bail out now, just when it looked as though the first of their ransom money was going to come through. Pure madness.

"We're not going anywhere Shelley, understood?"

"No, it's not bloody understood Jack! I say we split now while we're still ahead. We'll move to another town. Start again."

"We're perfectly safe in Sevilla, Shelley and we'll stay put until all the other families have paid up, is that so difficult a concept for you to grasp?"

"But we won't have any other families to bribe if the rebels show. They'll take over our operation completely!"

Tired of bickering, Jack wrapped his arm over Shelley's narrow shoulders.

"Have I ever let you down before old pal?"

"Several times."

"Well not this time, I promise you. This time everything is going to work out just fine. Now let's say we make a start on clearing up the courtyard. The place is in such a terrible state."

"It's your mess. You clear it up," Shelley replied, brushing away Jack's arm and stomping off toward his room. Jack let him go. He wasn't concerned. He knew his old friend well enough by now to know that in a few hours, like clockwork, he would turn up again and apologize for his minor outburst. Until then Shelley would use those hours to sulk and that was fine with Jack.

~ ~ ~

It had taken just over two hours to clear away the mess which had been left in the courtyard from the previous evening's festivities. Without Shelley to talk with, Jack had grown quickly bored by nine that morning and had turned instead to his other best friend.

"Ah, where would I be without you," he mumbled to himself as he ambled down the chapels wide central isle, lightly tapping the numerous bottles of wine which had been placed along the wooden pews with his forefinger. The catholic nuns had long gone. The Convento del Santo Ecce Homo, founded 1620, had been abandoned five years previous due to a serious lack of funds and now its cosy chapel had come to serve as an excellent wine cellar.

Reaching the altar, long since stripped of all its silver, Jack stopped, his final footsteps echoing through the building. In his current, difficult situation it would have been understandable if at that very moment Jack had fallen to his knees and burst into prayer. But Jack being Jack had never believed in all that wishful nonsense and instead picked up the nearest bottle of red wine, his strong hands quickly pulling out its stubborn cork.

"Jack?"

He'd heard Sebastian's footsteps long before he'd even spoken.

"Come to hear my sins?" he replied.

"We don't have that much time Jack, I just came to apologize for earlier on, didn't mean to storm off like that."

Jack smiled.

"No need to say sorry...Care for a drink?" he went on, offering Shelley the bottle. Shelley refused.

"My God we have got it bad today haven't we?"

"We still need to talk Jack, I mean seriously talk."

"Well, if we must."

Both men found themselves an empty pew and took a seat.

"Can't begin to imagine what it is that you want to talk about though," Jack went on sarcastically, holding the bottle to his mouth, a single drop of red wine landing across his white shirt as he took his first swig.

Ordinarily, this fresh stain would have stood out a mile, but after last night's party it blended easily in amongst the other beer, cigarette and smoke stains the shirt had quickly accumulated.

"You must have heard the rumours which are flying around town, Jack?" Shelley began. He was going to have one last crack at trying to change his friend's mind. One last throw of the dice before he would have to make his own difficult decision. Should he stay with Jack in Sevilla and risk almost certain slaughter? Or should he go with Greco and feel like a traitor for the rest of his days? Either way time was running out. Greco's bus would arrive in the main square in less than four hours and Shelley's mind was still torn. As he'd posed the question Jack had almost spat out the wine he'd been drinking.

"Of course I've heard the bloody rumours Shelley!" he yelled.

"But that's all they are, careless rumours. The rebels are all talk, idle gossip cleverly designed to make us want to run; to make gullible fools like you want to run!" he finished, his face having turned quite red, quite quickly.

"There's no need to talk to me like that Jack!" Shelley snapped. He wasn't really angry. He'd second guessed the sort of reaction he was going to get and had prepared his temper thoroughly for such an eventuality.

"Well, what do you expect man? How many times have we to go over this same topic? You're starting to bore me Shelley, you really are."

"Well one of us has to worry about this sort of thing. Christ if it was left to you we'd of been dead long ago!"

Jack sighed, resting the bottle between his knees. His friend did have a valid point. Jack had never been one for details. It was usually left to Sebastian to handle travel arrangements, payments, accommodation and all the other tedious necessities that were required when one of his outrageous schemes was about to go into operation. And yes there had been occasions where Shelley's common sense and practical grounding had got them out of trouble.

"Oh, lighten up for heaven's sake!" Jack retorted, knowing Shelley was right and hating the fact.

"And how do you know the rebels are all bluff Jack? Can you tell me that? Christ! Don't you hear the gunfire each night? It's getting closer by the hour!"

"Just because..."

"Just because of what?"

"Well because, because...Now Shelley I just have this feeling that everything will turn out good, alright?"

"No Jack, it's far from alright!"

"Look, if the rebels were going to attack they would have done so by now. The very fact that we have all these rumours flying around tells me that it's all fancy...You see?"

Shelley didn't see. He could detect no logic in Jack's speech and now Greco's bus was looking more and more appetizing. "And the gunshots?"

"Now everybody in Colombia carries a weapon Shelley. That doesn't prove a damn thing!" Jack replied, leaning forward. He hadn't brushed his teeth from last night and his breath smelt foul as he spoke:

"Look, you fetch the Walker ransom tomorrow evening, right?"

"Right."

"Well, we'll have over a hundred grand in our pockets. More than enough loot to hire extra men if and when the rebels do decide to pay our town a visit, which they won't. Don't you get it? That means we can sit back and relax. Count all our lovely dough and wait for the other two families to pay up! Wonderful stuff!"

"I'm not so sure Jack; the rebels are a pretty tasty bunch."

Jack sprang to his feet.

"Oh, God give me strength," he bellowed, already facing the altar. Sebastian could be a good pal and everything, but Christ he could be a real bore at times too. A real wet blanket.

"And what about your son Jack? What about him?"

"I've arranged a second bus to collect him this very afternoon if you must know...Samuel will be fine, just fine," he lied.

"Well, I suppose that's one good thing you've managed to sort out."

"So does that mean we're friends again? Can we now just stick to the original plan and put all this foolish talk of running away to the very back of our minds, where it rightly belongs?"

Sebastian was busy biting his lower lip. Jack was a good man, the very best sort of friend, but at times like this Sebastian's love for the chap could quickly turn to hate and a cold feeling of distance split them as if they'd never even been friends.

"I need a few minutes to think it over Jack," he replied, now cradling his head in both hands. Greco or Jack? The names continued to spin around his tired brain and didn't look like stopping for some time to come.

"You'll worry yourself to death one of these days Sebastian," Jack went on, already starting back down the aisle, the bottle of wine still clutched in his hand.

"On your head be it, Jack Locke," Shelley muttered after him.

"But isn't it always?" Jack quipped, pushing open the chapel doors and stepping back out into the courtyard. From now on Shelley could have all the precious time he wanted.

8

Fairfax Hall

"Any second now lads," the small boy spoke, sitting before the family's large, flickering television set. He was talking to his small army of toy soldiers, carefully laid out before him.

It was ten past four. Samuel had just finished school and on a Monday watching cartoons had become as compulsory as Math, English or any of those other tiresome subjects that he'd have to sit through each day. He sat with a carton of juice in one hand, waiting patiently for all the boring adverts to end and for his favourite cartoon to start. He'd been waiting almost five, long minutes when something called a newsflash had appeared on screen.

As it did, Sam had dropped his carton of juice. His mother had warned him many times about drinking juice without a glass and now their nice, new carpet was soaked.

"Dad," he whispered, his eyes stuck on the flickering screen and the photo of his dad.

He could hear the newsreader talking quickly over the image and Samuel shuffled closer toward the table in his eagerness to catch every word: 'Mr. Locke, forty one, was today jailed for ten years for his part in last week's audacious diamond heist. Looking calm and relaxed he was led away from the Old Bailey and bundled into a waiting police van.'

Samuel's tiny hand reached out and touched the screen. The reporter was still speaking but he was no longer interested in what the lady had to say. He was too busy watching the van that was now trying to navigate its way through the mob of other reporters; flashlights exploding into each of its darkened windows as it eventually managed to free itself. Again the screen flickered, and as it did the room which Samuel sat in also began to flicker. The dream now took a leap. The TV and lounge quickly vanished. Samuel could see a second room now, a large library, filled to its rafters with books of all ages and all descriptions. He was older too. He was ten. His father would appear soon, Shelly too. It wouldn't be long. He'd had the same dream many times down the years and it always played out the same. Deep in sleep, Samuel's body twitched.

It was midnight and Fairfax Hall was asleep. Samuel was stood alone in the library, the last chime from the room's Grandfather clock still echoing about its leather bound walls. For a moment he watched as the heavy rain lashed against the library's solitary window, and then began to shiver a little as the storm's icy chill crept slowly through his thin pyjama bottoms.

He stood quietly, his tired head cocked skyward. Before him, a thick chard of faint moonlight fell through the library window, spilling across the room's reading table and lapping over his naked feet. He didn't notice. His eyes were fixed on the ceiling, studying the strange hump that bulged at its centre. He completely missed Webster's elongated figure too which hovered close by, just beyond the reading table.

The Hall's butler had been watching Samuel for some time and was now waiting for that right moment to approach. The lad looked so engrossed he didn't want to scare him. Still oblivious, Samuel continued to study the ceiling. The hump above was located in direct proportion to the library's reading table that cowered some distance beneath, maybe a fraction longer. Samuel thought of a time when his father had taken him to the London Natural History Museum. He recalled the skeleton of a large humpback whale which had been hung from the museum's ceiling and this new wonder was easily comparable.

"You know, curiosity did kill the cat Master Locke."

Samuel almost died. Silently, Webster had left his shadows. He was now standing a few inches from where Samuel stood, his long, grey face looming large before him.

"You shouldn't be in here young Samuel," Webster continued, his thick grey eye-brows rising and falling in direct correlation with each spoken word. It was very funny to watch, especially for a ten year old. They each resembled two giant slugs which had been stapled to his forehead. Samuel couldn't help but smile.

"Is there something funny?"

"No."

"I know what you've been looking at. I've been watching you."

"I wasn't looking at anything," Samuel replied, a little afraid of the butler despite his comical appearance. "You must be mistaken," he continued, quickly realizing how foolish he sounded and wishing he'd just kept his mouth shut. Webster smirked.

"Do you even know what it is? That great big hump up there in the roof?"

Samuel shrugged. He didn't have a clue. Even his father had refused point blank to enlighten him. Webster again smirked. It wasn't a pleasant sight either. Three of his front teeth were missing and the rest looked decayed. Still grinning, the butler then took a seat at the reading table, his long legs stretching out beneath the table, almost covering its entire width.

"We have Gypsies who live on Fairfax land young Samuel. They've been here for generations. They were here long before I arrived. Long before my predecessor too. They keep all their cash stored right up there," Webster rattled on, one of his long and bony fingers now pointing to the hump. "For a dent that size to have formed, one can only guess as to how much has been collected down the years. Of course I've never been allowed to see it all for myself. I'm just the butler. Lord Fairfax has the key to that particular room. Only himself and a few of the Romany are allowed to enter."

Samuel pictured a treasure trove, a magical, glittering catacomb.

"Does your father know you're down here Samuel?" Webster continued, now looking directly at him.

Again, Samuel shrugged.

"You do realize that theft is a very serious crime Samuel. I've known your father for some years. Lord Fairfax is broke you see and I fear that Mr. Locke is putting silly thoughts into William's head."

Samuel was lost. Jack had snatched him from his mother only four days previous. Fairfax Hall was still new to him and he didn't think his young brain could cope with any more riddles.

"I …I…I don't think I follow," Samuel managed to mumble. Webster paused and Samuel thought he noticed something like compassion creep across the butler's face.

"Oh, go back to your bedroom young Master. Take no notice of me. I'm just an old man who's afraid of change. Go to sleep child and don't concern yourself with things which are out of your control. It's the best way. I'm sure your father has all our best interests at heart. I'm sure of it."

Samuel wasn't so sure. He missed his mother something terrible. Almost a week had passed since Jack had brought him to Fairfax Hall and still his father had refused to give him a simple explanation.

"Well, did you hear what I said? Go back to your room and I'll forget that I ever saw you. Do we have an understanding?"

Slowly, Samuel nodded. He didn't want to argue with the man and so, turning quickly, he left the library. Tomorrow, he promised himself, he would have words with his father.

~ ~ ~

"And through here is the main study. Dash it! If the blasted thing would open that is," Lord Fairfax cursed, pressing his slender shoulder hard against the study door. "I blame the woodworm! Buggered the locks, you know?" he rambled on. The door refused to budge. Jack wasn't surprised. It was only breakfast and already Fairfax was drunk on cheap whiskey. Jack had actually smelt his old friend that morning before seeing him.

"Here, let me," Jack spoke with authority, shoving the unsteady Lord to one side while pressing his own weight against the door's worn frame. The woodworm didn't stand a chance with Jack. The door flew open at once.

"Good man Jack! Top stuff!"

"Nothing to it, William."

Samuel shared a quick smile with his father. Dutifully, Jack smiled back. He was in a good mood for once that morning and Samuel was hoping to pick his brains soon after their meeting with Lord William. He would have done it over breakfast except that his father had been raving on about the great British countryside and how good it was to get decent air in the lungs.

"Ah! My favourite room Jack. Isn't she lovely?"

Samuel hovered close to his father as they both entered the new room. However, he didn't share Lord William's enthusiasm. Indeed, the study reminded Samuel of Fairfax himself. It was small, narrow, and had a strange smell about it. It was nothing special at all.

A large and very disorganized bookshelf sat against the far wall. To their immediate right an old piano, with several of its keys missing, was facing a large, half opened bay window, its net curtains billowing into the drab looking study.

"Well, what do you think?" Fairfax questioned, all excited as only small men who haven't quite grown up can get excited.

"It smells funny," Samuel whispered.

Jack smiled. Fairfax ignored the criticism.

"The room could do with a little fresh air," Jack continued in a more diplomatic fashion.

"It smells like old farts," Samuel went on, pushing his luck.

"You should remind your dear son that he is a guest. I could charge the blighter rent!"

"What a daft idea. I'm only ten. Ten year olds don't pay rent!"

"Well they should! Still, you're right. The place does pong a bit," Fairfax conceded, staggering toward the bay window. "I'll sort it child. Not a problem."

Having wrestled his way through the billowing curtains, Fairfax soon forced open the bay window. The window itself led out onto a small balcony. Both Samuel and Jack followed the lord outside.

"I do love the view from here boys," Fairfax now slurred, hovering close to the balcony railings, a little too close for Jack's liking.

"Be careful old son. Those railings look about as reliable as you."

"Don't you worry Jack. Fairfax Hall wouldn't do me any harm. She's been in the family for generations."

Gently, Jack placed a hand across William's unsteady back.

"We should go back inside. We can take a seat and have ourselves a good chat."

"I'm fine old chum, really I am."

"Samuel. Go and fetch Fairfax a chair from the dining room."

"On my own?"

"Well of course on your bloody own! Would you like me to hold your hand?"

"But..."

Jack's broad forehead suddenly creased.

"Scoot!"

Quietly, Samuel left the balcony.

"He's a good boy Jack. You shouldn't bawl at him like that. I made the same mistake with my own son. I hardly see him now."

"I'm afraid Samuel has been living with his mother for too long. He needs to toughen up."

Fairfax didn't reply. Out of all the people Jack knew, and he knew an awful lot, Lord Fairfax owned the shortest attention span. The ageing aristocrat had already turned his back on Jack, his frail eyes now searching ahead, across the vast manor lawns, a crispy white in the early morning, and on toward the thick forest that encircled Fairfax Hall.

"I never thanked you for letting us stay," Jack spoke.

"What was I supposed to do? Turn you both away? You don't have a pot to piss in."

Jack didn't reply. The truth hurt.

"Besides, I need your help too. At the moment I have my own financial worries."

"You could always open the Hall to the public. That would bring in some lolly."

"I may be old Jack but I'm far from senile! Fairfax Hall is on its last legs. Only a madman would pay to loiter about this wreck! I had to flog all the valuables!"

Jack stayed silent. Fairfax turned his attention back toward the distant line of forest.

"You know why you're here Jack. Stop playing dumb."

As he spoke, Fairfax began to watch with some interest the thin plumes of smoke that snaked their way up through the distant trees.

"I'm not a young man anymore William. I'm not sure my body would be up to the task."

Fairfax smiled.

"Don't talk nonsense. You're as fit as anyone I know."

"What you have in mind is very risky old friend. If you steal from Gypsies they'll simply make it their life's mission to track you down and slit your throat open! I know. I've had dealings with Romany in the past. They don't give two hoots about the law."

Again, Fairfax smiled.

"You both have something in common then?"

"Now look William. You'll be breaking a verbal contract that's been held in your family for generations. You should keep that in mind," Jack continued looking very grave.

"I don't have any option left Jack. Fairfax Hall is lost. At least with their cash I can start a new life in some other country. I'll reward you handsomely too Jack. I know you need the cash. You have a fine son to support now. Don't forget that."

That much was true and the offer was very tempting. Deep in thought, Jack's eyes had begun to watch the smoke plumes too, only he was looking more to their source. In amongst the trees he could see the fires that were responsible, but not the Romany men who'd lit them.

"The Romany will leave Jack. It's just a matter of when. They'll take every last penny with them too! You know it Jack."

"Have you tried reasoning with them?"

"Of course I have. What a bloody silly question. But the community is split. The older generation is happy to stay. It's their kids who want out," William continued. "I can't blame them for wanting shot of Fairfax Hall. There's nothing here for them," he finished looking even more resigned.

"Well, your words must carry some weight William," Jack pressed, running a careful eye across his friend's dark olive complexion. Fairfax was quick to notice his interest and forced a smile.

"My Mother was a real beauty Jack. A true Romany princess as my father liked to quip. But I'm still only a half-breed to them. They don't listen to my opinions Jack."

"Such an ungrateful bunch. If it wasn't for your father they'd have no home!" Jack continued, beginning to dislike the gypsies more and more.

"Well, that's not quite true. He was never quite comfortable with the idea. It was all down to my mother. He was desperately in love. What other option did he have but to let her family settle on Fairfax land? Besides, they paid their way. They paid very well too. Father never asked where it came from either!"

Jack chuckled.

"And here was I thinking your pops was some sort of frantic romantic!"

"Now cash is cash Jack," William replied, sharing a quick smile with his old friend.

"But like I said, if the Romany leave now I'll have nothing. It's me or them."

"Dad."

Both men broke off their conversation to find Samuel standing beside the room's open door, a large brown chair now resting obediently beside his right thigh.

"Good lad Samuel. Good lad," Jack praised, strolling over to his son.

"Is everything okay Dad?"

"Okay? Why yes, of course everything is okay. Why do you ask?"

Samuel didn't reply. He was looking a little way beyond Jack's shoulder to where Lord William was stood. Slowly, Jack turned to follow his son's curious gaze.

"He's crying Dad. Lord William's crying."

Much to Jack's surprise, William had now slumped to the foot of the railings, a flood of tears already streaming through his fingers and onto the balcony floor. Far behind him the twisting plumes of smoke were still quite visible spiralling into the early morning sky. Jack sighed heavily.

"I think it's high time I set you straight on a few things, young Sammy. Do you think you're big enough now for a man to man chat?"

Without hesitation, Samuel nodded. Maybe now he'd explain why he'd been taken from his mother and dragged to this strange place.

"Good. Then help me get William back inside and then we'll talk. That okay with you boy?"

Again, Samuel nodded. Leaving the chair to fend for itself, both father and son then made their way cautiously over to where William sat.

~ ~ ~

Shelley had been sitting in the lounge alone for over ten minutes before Catherine returned holding the small wooden picture frame to her chest.

"Catherine," Shelley began nervously. "Catherine my dear. I don't think this is at all healthy."

"He's gone too far this time. He's gone way too far. You know it Sebastian."

She'd stopped crying some time ago. The tearstains were still visible across her cheeks and as she took a seat opposite Shelley, she bought

133

out a clump of used tissues from her apron pocket. Dabbing her cheeks tenderly she continued:

"You must stop him Shelley. Do you understand? He can't be allowed to keep

Samuel! He belongs with me. I'm all he's known!"

Shelley had arrived at Catherine's small terrace cottage not long after midday. Her cottage sat opposite the village church and as she'd opened the door to her modest home the church bells had begun to chime the afternoon's arrival. Jack had whisked Samuel off the previous day and now Catherine was adamant that Shelley rescue him from Jack's irresponsible clutches.

"Now Catherine, he won't let any harm come to the boy. He loves the child. You know this as well as I do," Shelley persisted, hoping his words would somehow soothe Catherine's mood. If anything her expression soured even more. Just whose side was he on?

"Samuel belongs with his Mother," came the firm reply. "Jack can barely take care of himself. You know I'm right Shelley," she continued looking him straight in the eye, daring him to disagree. Knowing she was right, Shelley nodded his head in agreement. He couldn't really argue with her. Snatching Samuel had been unforgivable and stupid. As usual with Jack, he'd been the last to know.

"He only wanted the occasional weekend with the boy. That's all he ever asked for, Catherine," Shelley began to mutter. "I'm sure he only acted out of frustration. You know Jack. He just doesn't think at times. He'll come to his senses soon enough."

Catherine's eyes now fixed on him. She was a delicate little creature. At the best of times she hardly ever spoke above a whisper, even in her most animated moments. But now her temper was up. What a stupid thing to have said!

"Are you blaming me for this Sebastian?" she blasted, taking him quite by surprise. "Are you really trying to pin this one on me?'

"Now, Catherine..."

"Don't you even dare. Don't you even try to turn this one around on me," she continued, her pale neck and cheeks quickly turning a light red with rage.

"He had no right to take Samuel from me. None!"

She was about to cry for a second time that evening. Shelley had had a belly full of her waterworks already and decided it was better to stay quiet.

"I just want you to bring him back. That's all Sebastian. I just want Samuel home," she went on, managing to keep her tears at bay. Shelley nodded. Despite his loyalty to Jack, he couldn't sit and watch Catherine suffer like this. The truth was he'd always been rather fond of Jack's best girl.

"You know where they are, don't you Sebastian?"

Of course he knew where Jack had taken Samuel. Fairfax Hall had been a favourite retreat of Jacks for many years. Shelley had never stepped foot inside the place himself, but he knew it would only take him an hour's drive or so to reach her dilapidated gates.

"Yes, of course I'll bring the boy back," he whispered, taking a seat next to her and glancing down toward the framed photo.

"He's got Jack's eyes. Don't you think?"

"Stop it Sebastian. Don't try to change the subject. You always do this when Jack does something stupid."

"Was that a yes?"

Catherine rolled her eyes.

"Yes, I know. Samuel has beautiful blue eyes. I just hope he grows up to have better sense than Jack," she quipped, managing to force a thin smile. For a moment they sat in silence. The cottage was small but well decorated. Whatever cash Jack had wasted over the years, he'd always seen to it that Catherine and the boy had been well provided for. He had to give the man credit for that at least.

"I gave everything up for that man," Catherine began to whisper. "I was such a silly, silly girl."

Slowly, Shelley wrapped a comforting arm about her shoulder.

"Now you shouldn't go beating yourself up like that Catherine. Did you really stand a chance against Jack's persistence?"

The simple answer was no. There weren't a lot of people who could resist Jack's charms. Especially not a sheltered young girl who'd barely stepped foot outside her native village. No. Jack should have known better and left well alone.

"He always said you deserved better than him," Shelley continued, hugging her even tighter. "He always said it in jest but deep down I suspect he really believed this, Catherine."

"Are you so sure Sebastian?"

"Would I lie to my favourite girl?"

Catherine smiled.

"No Sebastian. You wouldn't lie to me. Not you Sebastian."

Resting her head into his chest, Catherine continued:

"Sebastian?"

"Yes Catherine?"

"Are you happy these days?"

Shelley chuckled. What an absurd question.

"Well, to be perfectly honest, Catherine, I never give the subject much thought. I don't have the time. I'm too busy clearing up after Jack."

"It's just that you look so lonely of late. I can see it in your eyes Sebastian. It's difficult to hide such a look. Maybe you need to find yourself a nice girl. You could do with the company."

"Oh, really. Is that what you think?"

She was looking into his large brown eyes now, watching the emptiness.

"Do you have a girl, Sebastian?"

Shelley pressed his lips gently across her brow, only this time lingering a little longer than was comfortable.

"You know. There was a time Catherine. A long while ago. When we all first met. I often wondered what would have happened if I'd asked you out first."

Catherine blushed.

"Shelley darling."

"No. I didn't stand a chance, did I? Not against Jack."

Slowly, Catherine placed her little finger across Shelley's lips.

"Just bring Samuel back Sebastian. Just bring my boy back home."

~ ~ ~

The ground felt soft underfoot. Samuel tried to clear some of the collected mud from his boot but found it had already frozen in the short space of time it had taken him to reach the fields beyond the manor lawns. It was raining too, a dirty, filthy downpour. Quite soon the fields would become nothing more than a giant quagmire.

He looked toward the line of forest that grew still some distance away and then back toward

Fairfax Hall, the lights from its distant windows all but a collection of tiny flickers. He'd left his father and Lord William talking alone in the library over an hour ago. Despite it being first light, he was certain they'd still be talking, sipping happily from their sherry glasses as they went along.

Samuel had listened intently to their conversation. At first he'd kept to the library's shadows in fear that his presence would somehow stop their tales. They'd talked about many things and many strange places. They'd talked well into the small hours about money and women and other things he didn't quite understand yet, until finally their rambling conversation had settled on the Romany. The Gypsies fascinated him. He didn't know why for sure, only that their life seemed so far removed from his own.

Leaving the field, Samuel now took his first tentative steps into the forest proper. With the light from his small pocket torch, he quickly found a pathway through the pressing trees. At one point he left the track and for a moment every sinew in his body begged him to turn back. He stayed. There were lights ahead of him. He could see them clearly through the many branches and leaves that crowded him. And there were figures too. It wasn't just his imagination playing careless tricks. He could see the shadows of men passing quickly before these lights.

Slowly, Samuel began to pull his camera free from his backpack. In that moment he thought of his father. He could hear Jack talking about deserts and jungles. He could hear Jack describing his first meetings with strange, far away tribes and with each of these recollections Samuel knew he didn't want to be anywhere else.

Once again his eyes focused on the lights and in particular those figures shifting amongst them. Carefully, his hands began to stroke the camera's thin leather strap and for a second time Samuel thought he understood his father. He had a sense of some future life awaiting him. A life filled with travel and adventure. And it felt good.

He started toward the Romany camp. Soon, he could hear real voices. He understood the words that came to him above the sound of the rain and the rustling of trees, but not the accents that covered them. His father was going to be impressed. He was sure. He was going to shoot some very fine images that morning and then, just maybe, he would be his father's son at last.

"What's your name child?"

In his fright, Samuel nearly dropped the camera. Clutching its strap, he spun off to his left hoping to find the source of this sudden voice. He found only more trees. Then, as he began to look closer, off to his extreme left, he discovered a tiny clearing bathed in faint moonlight.

"Did you hear what I said? I asked your name child. You really shouldn't be here. This is Romany land."

The voice was soft, feminine and foreign. He thought of his Aunt Iris who lived in Galway but knew this accent wasn't quite the same as hers. He began to study the clearing more closely, daring the owner of this strange voice to appear. She didn't. Not quite. He could see a slim figure living on the clearing's edge but not the face that would give it life. So he waited.

"Don't you have a name? Is that the problem here? Didn't your mammy name you?"

"My name's Samuel."

She stepped forward as he replied. Her hair was long and dark and wild, her light, green eyes quite calm in comparison. She stood semi naked now in the centre of the silver clearing, her brown and voluptuous figure barely covered by a flimsy white gown.

"Samuel? That's funny. I have an elder brother by the name of Samuel. You know, I have a younger sibling too. We call him Sean. He likes to run and hide from us at times. That's why I'm here. To find him. Have you seen a wee young scamp called Sean?" the girl suddenly yelled, racing across the clearing and diving behind a nearby bush. Samuel flinched at the unexpected movement and almost bolted himself.

"Got you!"

A moment later and the girl reappeared, only this time holding a young boy of about three tightly under her right arm. The boy giggled and squirmed as best he could but could not escape.

"Don't be frightened Samuel. You're not in any trouble. You shouldn't listen to all the talk about Romany you know. We're a good people."

"I'm not afraid," Samuel lied. "And I haven't heard any bad talk."

Still struggling to keep Sean tucked under her arm, the girl smiled. She was more than simply pretty. Those words didn't do her justice. She was beautiful.

"Is that your camera Samuel? It looks mighty fancy."

"It's my father's. He lets me borrow it."

"And you've come all this way just to take our snaps?"

Samuel shrugged.

"I think so."

"Well, that's very flatterin' of you. Isn't that nice Seany?"

"No!" the boy yelled back, quickly breaking into another fit of giggles as he did.

"Take no notice Samuel. Sean doesn't know any other words yet. Do you, you wee scamp?"

"No! No! No!"

Slowly, Samuel began to edge away.

"Hey! Where do you think you're goin'? You just got here!"

"I think... I think I have to leave..."

"Oh, don't be so daft now. You've no need to be scared. I told you. We're a good set of folk down here. Wouldn't you like to take some snaps of our home Sammy? Wouldn't you like that?"

Samuel found himself caught in two minds and simply couldn't reply.

"My name's Christina by the way," the girl continued. She smiled as she replied. A perfect white beam. "Well? Would you like to see our home or not? I haven't got all the day to be standin' around an' chattin' you know? Make your mind up!"

"I guess so."

As Samuel replied, another perfect white smile lit up Christina's entire face.

"Ah now, did you hear that Seany? We've made a new friend!"

"No! No! No!"

"And does your Daddy like to see your snaps Samuel?"

"I think so. I mean he's never seen any of my shots before. But I hope he'll like these ones."

"Then come on with you. Let's go and take a look together. You ready?"

Samuel quickly nodded. Beginning to smile himself, he followed Christina and her still captive brother through what remained of the wood to the very edge of their home.

~ ~ ~

Shelley banged his impatient fist against the door's solid oak for a fifth consecutive time. He was ready to try his luck with the servant's entrance when the sound of many rusted bolts coming from beyond the door's worn panelling stopped him. It was still early morning. Shelley had left Catherine in the small hours and now he felt very tired and quite irritable. Slowly, the door opened and Webster's long face appeared.

"Yes, can I help you at all sir?"

"I'm looking for Jack Locke."

Webster had been the Fairfax butler for nearly fifty years and he'd known Jack on and off for a good ten of those.

"Mr. Locke is in the library. He's as pissed as a newt. Are you a friend?"

"Yes. But I'm having second thoughts."

"Shall I tell him that..."

"Save it."

Letting his jacket and gloves flop over Webster's outstretched arms, Shelley pushed his way past the ageing butler and into the lobby proper.

"I say sir, that was very impolite!"

"Yes it was. You're quite right. I apologize. Now, if you can just take me to the library I'll behave myself. Do we have a deal?"

Webster drew in a deep breath. He could feel his temper slipping but duty kept him in check.

"Very well. Follow me sir."

With that, both men made their way through the Hall's numerous corridors. Within minutes

Shelley was standing inside the main library come brewery.

"Sebastian! Is that really you Sebastian? What a pleasant surprise. What brings you all..."

"Shut up Jack!"

Jack had just managed to lift himself up from off the library carpet when Shelley had burst in looking all hot and flustered. Webster had already retired quietly from the room.

"You look vexed Sebastian. What's the matter?" Jack continued, trying to find one final bottle of unopened champagne in amongst the emptied ones.

Shelley ignored him and began to scour the room. It wasn't long before he noticed a body slumped next to the library's historical section.

"Is that Fairfax? Is he dead?"

"Don't think so."

"Are you sure? He isn't moving."

"Would you like some Champagne Sebastian?"

Jack was now sitting at the table. He'd managed to find the one remaining full bottle and looked very pleased with himself.

"Where's Samuel? Where is he?"

"Are you sure you wouldn't like a small tipple?"

Shelley's eyes narrowed

"Do you want me to lose my temper Jack? I've just spent over three hours comforting your ex-wife and I don't need any more stress. You had no right to take the boy from her."

"I had every right damn it man! He's my bloody son isn't he?" Jack suddenly exploded, picking up one of the sherry glasses and hurling it inches past Shelley's head. Shelley didn't flinch. He was used to Jack's tantrums.

"Catherine is beside herself."

"Well, the woman is a born worrier. She'll get over it."

"I hate to be the one to remind you my dear disillusioned man, but you're flat broke and young boys need to be provided for!"

Jack grinned, his big blue eyes lighting up. Shelley had seen this sort of smile before and it always made him feel very uncomfortable.

"Oh, Jack. What are you up to now?"

"Flat broke am I?"

"Well, you have a plan?"

Another devilish grin.

"Would you like to share it?"

Jack sat himself bolt upright, running a quick hand through his fine blonde hair. Clearing his throat, he continued:

"Fairfax and I have reached an agreement!"

"Oh really? I'm surprised you could both string a sentence together."

Jack chuckled. He was very much intoxicated.

"Have you noticed anything strange about the room Sebastian?"

"You mean apart from yourself?"

"Sebastian!"

Rolling his eyes, Sebastian began to search the room. Only Fairfax seemed out of place. Shelley had visited Fairfax Hall many times down the years but this was still his first foray into the library.

"Now, I'm in no mood for any of your silly games Jack! I'm a grown man of thirty - eight years!" he blasted. "Jack? Damn it man. Are you even listening?"

Jack's devilish grin was still present although now his big blue pearls were looking skyward.

"Jack Locke will you please answer me!"

"Tell me Sebastian. Did you even spot the ceiling on your way in?"

"I'm sorry?"

"The ceiling Sebastian. Heaven's above man! I had you down as more observant."

Slowly, Shelley began to follow Jack's gaze.

"My word!" he gasped quickly, his eyes having settled on the large hump which hung directly above their heads.

"I know Sebastian. I know."

"Whatever is the cause Jack? I've never seen a thing like it."

"Loot old boy. Good old fashioned lolly!"

"Loot! How much loot?"

"Lots and lots of loot. More than we could carry off by ourselves."

"And where on Earth did it all come from?" Shelley continued, his head remaining tilted backward as he spoke, studying the ceiling's strange hump as if its very belly was about to crack open and spill its contents all over their greedy heads.

"Why, the Gypsies of course!"

"Gypsies?"

"That's right. The Romany who live on Fairfax land. It's their cash. Every last penny. They've been hoarding it up there for generations. It's a surprise the bloody roof hasn't collapsed already. It's a neat little arrangement. William takes a small cut each month for rent. Of course he's never had to ask where the money comes from! And I do like that sort of thing! He let me in on the whole gig yesterday!"

"Good grief," Shelley replied, still eyeing the hump. "How much do you think there is?"

Jack shrugged. The question didn't seem important.

"Enough to start a new life. With that sort of cash we could hop and skip it to the Americas! We could live like bloody kings! You know, Samuel would have a great life Sebastian. The very best of everything," Jack went on, his tone simply bubbling with enthusiasm.

Shelley leant forward, his elbows resting against the table's chipped edge.

"Jack. I'm going to say this one last time old bean. Samuel belongs with his mother. I know you love the boy to pieces. I know this Jack. But a boy like your Sammy just doesn't belong with a pair of crooks like us. Christ man, the boy has a brain between his ears. He has a real future!"

Jack listened intently and then heaved a huge sigh. Once again Shelley was right and he always found it very irritating.

"Well, I'm afraid it's too late!"

"Too late?"

"That's right. Like I said. Fairfax and I have reached an agreement. We have a big van ready and waiting for us in the garage. All we have to do is load her up with the cash and then bugger off! Perfect!"

"And the Gypsies?"

"Sod them. They'll never find us in Brazil, Sebastian! It's the only plan left available. It's either scarper now or fight the bleeders for it. And you don't honestly think the Romany would leave all their loot here at Fairfax Hall when eventually they do decide skip town? Well? Do you?"

"Jack Locke. I do believe you have lost your mind this time."

"Oh stop fretting Sebastian. You can be such a bore at times. You really are a frightened little man are you not?"

"Where's Samuel?"

"He's in bed if you must know. Give me some credit. Despite what you all think of me I do know how to look after my own bloody son! I know my responsibilities. No cheap whiskey after nine and in bed before sunrise! Simple!"

"Oh Jack."

At that very moment the library doors burst open and in stumbled Webster. He was out of breath and looked very worried.

"Webster! Have you come to join the party?"

"Shut up Jack," Shelley was quick to scold. "What's wrong Webster? You look awful."

Frantically dabbing his forehead with his old handkerchief, Webster composed himself before replying:

"It's the boy Mr. Shelley. He isn't in his room!"

"What? Samuel's missing?" Shelley blurted.

"Missing? But I sent the little bugger to bed myself! What do you mean he's missing?" Jack protested, his ego a little dented.

"It's worse than that Mr. Locke. I spotted young Samuel scampering off toward the woods not five minutes ago!"

"He was heading for the woods? I don't understand Webster," Shelley questioned.

Jack's smile suddenly returned. There was a new look in his eyes too. It was pride.

"The little blighter!"

"Will someone please tell me what is going on?" Shelley demanded. He was very much confused by this point.

"The little sod must have heard Fairfax and I talking about the Romany. He's gone off to see them for himself! How very brave!" Jack replied. "And here was I thinking I had a mummy's boy on my hands. How wrong a man can be at times."

And then, just as suddenly, Jack's expression stiffened, his wide forehead creasing into many different folds. Looking directly into Shelley's eyes he continued:

"Oh hell Sebastian. The little blighter's gone off to see the Gypsies! He'll ruin the entire plan! Fairfax! Webster! Someone fetch my bloody boots!" he began to bellow, leaping into the air. "We have a boy to catch!"

9

Gypsy Queen

One by one Samuel began to spot the Romany. He kept close to Christina as they appeared. She sensed his anxiety without having to look at him and simply held out her delicate hand. Together, they left the forest behind and stepped into a large clearing. There were twelve caravans in total, each of them hugging the clearing's haggard perimeter and half hidden amongst the trees and foliage that grew there. Sam had counted them long before he'd reached the forest's strange oasis.

"Are you alright Samuel?" Christina whispered, having taken her first steps into the clearing. "You look a little pale. There's no need to be worried. You're with friends now."

Sam welcomed the words, but they did little to stop the tightening in his stomach. At the very heart of the clearing several campfires burned. A small group of men hovered about the flames and only noticed the new arrivals when Christina and Samuel were but a few footsteps from the falling embers.

"Christina?" one of the men spoke, slowly climbing to his feet, a click in his knee accompanying the movement. "Who is this?"

Sam swallowed hard. The other men were beginning to stand also. These men were younger than the first and none of them bothered to smile as they turned to study the new child on their doorstep.

"He's called..."

"My name's Samuel," Samuel broke in, pretending he was his dad for a split second and imagining how Jack himself would have behaved in such a delicate situation.

"Samuel is it?" the eldest gypsy replied, looking deep into Samuel's eyes.

"That's right. My name's Samuel Locke."

"Locke?" the elderly gypsy continued. He sounded a little surprised. The surname was familiar. He'd come to know the name well over the past few days, but as yet he'd been unable to put a face to it. "Well, my name is Brendan. It's good to meet you, young Samuel."

"I found him in the woods, Father. He looked so lonely," Christiana went on, beginning to lower her younger brother to the ground. The boy was now unusually quiet and immediately hid himself behind her right thigh.

Slowly, Brendan held up his hand. He was a large man with receding grey and ginger hair. His forearms were very big and he still looked a powerful man despite his advancing years.

"Please be quiet now girl. I was talking to the boy."

As he spoke, the other Romany began to edge forward. They were a lot younger than Christina's father and now their own dark eyes seemed to burrow into Samuel's.

"We could take 'im with us," one of them then quipped. "We could stuff 'im in one of the wagons pappy. I'm sure nobody would miss a wee runt like 'im!"

"Fasten your gab Lyle. Can't you see you're makin' the lad nervous."

Samuel did feel very nervous at this point but did his best to hide any fear.

"He looks okay to me. Nothin' a bit of hard work wouldn't cure."

The other men laughed amongst themselves.

"What you doin' here boy?" Brendan continued. He looked around seventy. His skin was a dark brown and very wrinkled. A long and deep scar curved its way down and across his right cheek, almost kissing his lower lip. His voice was deep too, almost hypnotic.

"Well?"

"Well what?" Samuel replied, keeping up the front. He even surprised himself.

The Gypsy smiled.

"C'mon. I like you lad. You got balls. Would you like to see the inside of a real Gypsy wagon?"

Sam shrugged: "If you like."

He didn't want to do anything of the kind. He felt secretly terrified and all he could think of was taking flight into the woods. But already Christina had wrapped her arm about his shoulder and now it felt as though his only option was to follow.

"You not eating?"

Samuel toyed with what remained of his bacon and egg. His appetite had gone. He stared blankly back at Brendan. He didn't want to offend Christina's father but the breakfast he'd cooked for them both was making him feel sick.

"Perhaps you'd like a little more coffee Sammy?" Christina interrupted, feeling the tension and wanting rid of it.

"No. Really, I'm okay."

"Are you sure boy? You still look pale to me," Brendan continued, stuffing the last piece of bacon into his own mouth. Christina was already passing Samuel a fresh cup of black coffee.

"You look tired too. This will wake you up. After you've eaten we'll take you around the camp."

Samuel pushed his plate away. He didn't want to see the camp anymore. The spell had been broken. This adventure was supposed to have been a secret. Now the Romany knew he was here and for him the thrill had gone.

"Drink up Samuel. Before it turns cold," Christina spoke, looking at him sternly.

Brendan's caravan was larger in comparison to the others that ringed the clearing. Behind Brendan's right shoulder, at the very back of the caravan, the bedroom door stood open. Samuel noted the king-sized bed that lay beyond and began to yearn for the comfort and safety of his own bed. A tiny round window rose above the bed itself and, through it, Samuel could see the clearing and the trees that encircled it. It was still early, before eight, and the sky outside was a light grey in colour. The wind was up too and the tips of the trees were being made to sway violently just beneath the window's top ridge. Far beyond the forest, through its mesh of twisted branches, Samuel could see the faint houselights from Fairfax hall still blinking back at him.

"You know Christina. A wolf never leaves its pup alone for too long. It goes against nature," Brendan spoke, having left the breakfast table. He was standing before the caravan's door, his face pressed against its own window, a flurry of dead leaves occasionally blinding his view as he looked out onto the clearing.

"Is everything okay Father?"

"Fetch my rifle Christina."

"But what's wrong Pappy?"

"Nothing is wrong girl. Just do as I say."

Meanwhile Samuel had begun to stand.

"Money does queer things to queer folk. I know that much for a damned fact,"

Brendan went on, turning quickly to check on his daughter's progress. She was busy opening a large wooden chest that lay beside the breakfast table.

"Be quick now Christina. We have new guests to attend to."

Wanting to please her father, Christina quickened her pace. It wasn't long before she was crossing the caravan toward her him, the rifle held firmly in her hand.

~ ~ ~

Jack, Sebastian and Webster now stood at the clearing's edge watching the Romany. It had taken them nearly an hour to reach the Gypsy encampment and all three were very tired. Webster in particular had needed to stop several times during their trek through the wood. The difficult journey had even sobered Jack up a little. Shelley spoke first:

"We should have woken Fairfax. At least they know him!"

"Hold your nerve. We have Webster. They know Webster," Jack replied, still trying to catch his breath. The butler loitered a little way behind the two men. He seemed reluctant to leave the safety of the forest and simply hovered between two of its trees, the hood from his thick jacket pulled low across his forehead so that his eyes were only just visible as he glared back at his two compatriots. He stood tall, grey and motionless. He looked very much like one of the trees. Feeling his absence, Jack turned to find him.

"Webster. Are you still with us?"

"I'm still with you. I'm just waiting for them to call us first. Take my word. It's far better my way," Webster replied, sending a shiver down Shelley's back.

"I don't like this Jack. I don't like this one bit."

"Button it. I believe we've reached a delicate stage. We have a lot of cash riding on the next few minutes Sebastian. We can only hope that Sammy didn't hear about our plan and let it slip accidentally to the Romany. He is only ten after all."

Having spotted the new arrivals, the Romany were already making strides toward them, one or two even stepping through the fading bonfire itself in their eagerness to confront Jack and his two friends.

"Well, what do we say to them? They look bloody tough Jack!"

"Just leave the chat to me Sebastian."

Shelley understood. He kept quiet. This was Jack's territory now. For all the man's faults, Shelley knew there wasn't a better chap to have by your side in such a difficult situation. The first of the Romany, the eldest amongst them, now stepped forward.

Jack beamed a huge grin:

"Good morning to you sir!"

The Gypsy didn't flinch. He was shorter than Jack but very broad. His eyes were small like a weasels and he seemed to own a permanent scowl.

"My name is Jack Locke. This is my good friend Sebastian Shelley."

Shelley nodded toward the small mob.

"Now, we're not here to cause any trouble boys. Let's call it a brief social call. I'm looking for a small lad. He's a good-looking nipper who goes by the name Samuel Locke. He's my dear son you see and I'd very much like to have him home. There's a good chance he came by this way. Have you seen him?"

For a moment the Romany glanced at one another. Weasel eyes then spoke:

"We don't give a damn about your son mister. We don't give a damn about any city folk here. Best you leave before anyone gets hurt."

Shelley began to clench his fists. He was sure Jack was going to swing for the runt. To his credit, Jack remained calm. He simply smiled back and then replied:

"Now, that wasn't a very polite thing to say young man. A fella could take that as fighting talk. Perhaps you could try again?"

"I couldn't care less sir. You can takes it anyways you want."

Jack paused. For a moment the Champagne in his belly began to swell. He thought he was going to be sick but just managed to hold the liquid down. Clearing his throat he continued:

"In that case, perhaps I could talk to your boss."

"I'm the boss around here mister. You can talk to me."

"Well, I find that very hard to believe young man. To be honest, I don't think you have it in you. Now, is he around or not? I skipped breakfast this morning and I'm feeling all short tempered."

Weasel eyes smiled. The other Gypsies began to step closer, broadening their thick shoulders as they approached.

"We'll give you one more chance," Weasel eyes continued. "If you leave now I'll give you my word we'll not beat you both into a pulp. Is that understood?"

At that moment, as Jack was about to reply, a gunshot exploded above their heads. The Romany spun frantically around. Shelley almost fainted, while Jack remained calm, his keen eyes having found the shotgun's owner.

"It looks like things are hotting up Sebastian! How very exciting!"

Sebastian had also clapped eyes on the shotgun's owner. However, he didn't seem to share in Jack's enthusiasm. He was far more terrified than excited.

"He's got a bloody rifle!"

"He's got a bloody big rifle Shelley!"

The Romany had parted. Through them, some distance away at the clearing's edge, both Jack and Sebastian were now eyeing a large Gypsy wagon. Its doors were wide open and two new figures, Brendan and Samuel, were standing at the foot of its steps. Jack smiled.

"Well Shelley, I think we've found what we came for."

"At least he's safe Jack. We can be grateful for that at least,"

"And I think I know the bugger who's with him too Sebastian," Jack then mumbled, taking note of Brendan's receding ginger hair and ox-like frame.

"A Mr. Jack Locke I take it?" Brendan now shouted across the clearing, pushing Samuel to one side as he did. Jack stood himself to his full height. Filling his own lungs, he then bellowed back:

"That's right. I see you have my son. I have to thank you for taking care of him."

"My pleasure entirely Mr. Locke."

"What's the plan now Jack," Shelley whispered as Brendan began to stroll forward. Samuel followed gingerly behind. He was delighted but also a little worried at seeing his father again. He was going to get a rollicking for this one. Turning to Shelley, Jack replied:

"Nothing to worry about old son. We'll exchange a few pleasantries and then I'll break Samuel's bloody neck for getting us into this mess. Simple as that."

"Right. And then what?"

"And then Mr. Shelley we'll be gone within the hour, with as much Gypsy loot as we can carry!"

Shelley nodded.

"That okay with you?"

"Fine with me Jack. Fine with me."

"But first we have to rescue our little Sammy over there."

"It could be difficult Jack. The Romany look pretty ticked off. Do you think they know what you're up too?"

"Don't talk nonsense Sebastian. How could they possibly know?"

"It's just a feeling I'm getting Jack. Just a feeling that's all."

Jack narrowed his eyes. Something was troubling him too. He had a funny feeling about Samuel's new guardian. As Brendan neared, Jack suddenly recalled a bar brawl that had taken place one summer's evening back in Bethnal Green. He quickly spotted the deep scar that ran along Brendan's left cheek and was sure he'd known the man who'd given it to him. A small but stocky Scotsman popped into his head. He'd been called Robert or something like that. At once, Jack could see the scot with a pint glass in his hand. Now the glass was being thrown forward toward Brendan's glaring face, and then Brendan was sprawled across the pub's floor, blood everywhere. All this maybe ten or fifteen years previous.

"Jack Locke?"

"Yes."

Brendan gently patted at the scar that curled its way down his face. He was looking very closely at Jack as he did.

"Is everything okay?" Jack went on, pretty sure the Gypsy would recognise him.

"I think I've seen your face before Mr. Locke."

"Oh, really?"

"Yes, really. You sure we haven't met?"

Jack smiled, a salesman's grin.

"I wouldn't have thought so. I've known Fairfax for years but we've never been introduced. Perhaps I remind you of somebody else. Think carefully."

"Perhaps," Brendan replied, glancing toward Shelley. "Well, what can we do for you both? You've taken us quite by surprise. We haven't had city folk down here for a long time. It must be very important."

Again, Jack smiled.

"Well, I would have thought that was obvious."

It was Brendan's turn to smile now.

"You have a very brave son Mr. Locke. You ought to be proud."

Samuel looked vaguely up toward his father. He did his best to smile but found the task very difficult.

"I am proud. Very proud. I have a very fine son."

"He came all this way on his own you know. It's a long journey for such a wee chap."

"And I'm sure he'll be full of tales once we get him back," Jack finished, his eyes still fixed on Brendan.

"Fairfax Hall your home, is it sir?"

"No. We're just visiting. A weekend thing. Thought I'd show Samuel the pleasures of the English countryside. Now, if you would excuse us, we'll be on our way."

Jack went to pass Brendan. He was already reaching to grab Samuel when the Gypsy's shotgun blocked his path, its steel barrel pressing quickly into Jack's ribs. Jack froze. The surrounding Romany began to close in. On cue, Shelley stepped up beside him.

"I know you from somewhere Mr. Locke. I'm sure of it."

"Well, that's very nice to know."

"Fairfax Hall is such a grand looking building don't you think? Be a shame to see her turn to rubble."

Brendan's eyes were on the forest, through the forest. The early morning gloom had lifted and Fairfax Hall was quite visible now some distance beyond the trees.

"She is an impressive piece of work. I'll give you that," Jack replied calmly, trying to push the gun's barrel to one side. It was difficult because Christina's father was very strong.

"But it's what's inside that really counts isn't it Mr. Locke?" Brendan continued, keeping the gun steady. For the first time since their meeting Jack's smile had begun to slip a little.

"Inside? I'm not sure if I follow you sir."

Brendan chuckled.

"Don't play dumb fella. I know you're good pals with old Lord Fairfax. I have this on very good authority you see."

"And?"

"And I know what you've been up to. I know all about what you've been planning up there in that big old house of his. I know everything Mr. Locke. As a matter of fact we were going to pay both of you a visit very soon."

"Is that a fact?"

"Aye, that is a fact."

A pause. Again, Jack went to grab Samuel. Again, Brendan blocked his path with the shotgun. Stepping closer and talking directly into Jack's ear, so that Jack could smell the bacon and eggs on his breath, Brendan continued:

"Money does queer things to queer folk Mr. Locke. I know this much."

A second, longer pause. Lowering his voice, and now pressing his lips against Brendan's own right ear, Jack replied softly:

"Just let me pass Gypsy. Give me back the boy and they'll be no trouble."

"You're outnumbered Mr. Locke. Don't forget this."

"But I'm ready to take my chances Gypsy. I'm just about ready."

At that moment Webster appeared, having slid his way quietly through the gathered Romany. He shuffled quickly up to Christina's father.

"I still want my share of the money Brendan. Like you promised!"

"You bloody traitor!" Shelley barked suddenly, making a grab for the butler's scrawny throat. Jack stopped him just in time.

"Save it!"

"But Jack. He went behind your back! He told them all about your plans!"

"I said save it Sebastian!" Jack continued, pushing his best friend toward the Gypsies. Slowly, Brendan removed the shotgun.

"So you see Mr. Locke. I know all about your dealings with old Lord Fairfax. Webster has kept me well informed. We'll give him a grand reward too. More than Fairfax would have done for him."

"Then tell me straight. What do you want from me?"

"Well, I think it's what you want Jack. What you'll be wanting back safe and sound."

Samuel was already sobbing by this point. His Dad was looking very grave. Something else was wrong. Something else he didn't quite understand. It went beyond his leaving Fairfax Hall. Brendan's right hand was now resting across Samuel's head, his stubby fingers pressing quite hard into the boy's skull. Several times Samuel had winced.

"Just give me back the boy. That's all I ask."

"And then?"

"And then we'll be gone. And you can keep the bloody loot. Every last penny!"

Shelley was eyeing the Romany. There were five in total. They were strong looking lads but he was sure Jack could take them with a little help from himself. If they could just get their hands on the shotgun.

"Jack. Think about what you're doing."

"I've thought about it. Now be quiet Sebastian!"

"But we've been betrayed damn it!"

"Well? Do we have a deal?" Brendan went on, pushing the shotgun's barrel back into Jack's sore ribs.

"Yes. We have a deal. Now let Samuel pass."

Slowly, Brendan raised the shotgun. Quickly, Samuel darted into Jack's outstretched arms. Just as quickly, Jack scooped him up.

"Sammy? You okay boy?"

Very slowly, his eyes full of water, Samuel nodded his head.

"Everything's going to be alright now boy. You hear me? Don't you worry about a thing."

"And your loot?" Shelley chipped in, his eyes, like daggers, still on Webster.

"Bugger the loot Sebastian. We'll have other days to make cash."

"I should listen to your friend Mr. Shelley. He's talkin' a lot of sense," Brendan spoke, beginning to wave the other Romany away. One by one, they began to back off. "We'll be up to visit you pretty soon Mr. Locke. I suggest you leave every penny where you found it!" he finished with a greedy smile.

"I told you we had a deal Gypsy. You should know when to quit."

Unable to control his rage any longer, Shelley lunged for Webster. He had the butler by the neck for a few seconds until the Romany tore him off.

"Sebastian!"

"And what about Fairfax, Jack? Are we just going to leave him? He'll be ruined?"

"They won't touch Fairfax. Will you Gypsy?"

Brendan shrugged.

"No matter, we'll take William with us too. Just as soon as we get Samuel back to his mother."

"Well, at least you're starting to talk some sense!" Shelley said, pushing the last of the Romany off of him. As he finished speaking, Brendan pointed his shotgun toward the flustered Englishman.

"I'd keep that lip of yours buttoned up tight from now on if I were you. You're not out of these woods yet, mister."

As Brendan spoke, his eyes momentarily off Jack, Jack quickly slipped a little grey pouch into Samuel's jacket pocket. It was no bigger than a packet of crisps and had the initials JL embroiled in faint white across its skin.

"Dad?"

"Not a whisper Sammy! Do you understand?"

"But..."

"Not a whisper I said!"

"We'll be out of these woods pretty damn soon! Don't you worry about that Gypsy!" Shelley began to bark.

"Good. And don't think about coming back either of you!" Brendan roared back, raising the shotgun as he did and firing off a deafening volley. For a moment the entire forest came alive with the sound of panicked birds, their wings fluttering this way and that, a myriad of leaves and branches falling to the ground. Samuel wrapped his arms about his father and quickly burrowed his head into his chest.

"There was no need for that Brendan. I told you we had a deal."

"Just making sure Mr. Locke. Just wanted to be certain you understood," Brendan replied, patting Samuel's head as he did.

"Sebastian?"

"Yes Jack?"

"You ready?"

Sebastian threw Webster one final glance.

"Yes, Jack. I'm ready."

"Then let's go. I'm beginning to tire of these people."

"Right behind you."

Hugging Samuel even tighter to his chest, Jack then turned to leave. They'd gone a few paces across the clearing when Samuel, unable to hide his curiosity, spoke up:

"Dad?"

Wearily, Jack smiled.

"Yes Son."

"What did you put in my pocket?"

"Just a little present that's all. You'll see soon enough boy."

"But what sort of present?"

"The sort of present that will make you smile one day. When you're a lot older and you understand a little more."

"But..."

"Quiet now Samuel. You've had a busy day of it. It's time to get you home. You can talk all you want then. Is that a deal?"

"I guess."

"Good. Then put a sock in it."

With that, Samuel buried his head back into Jack's chest. Together, all three then re-entered the forest.

10

Best Laid Plans

Shelley had remained in church, his head turned toward the chapel's plain stone floor. He would turn sixty-four next birthday. As usual, Jack would throw his old friend a celebration and, as with every year, both men would drink too much, reminisce into the small hours and wake late the following day.

Shelley was feeling his age. He felt it in the stiffness of his joints, in the burden of remembrance, but mostly he could see her work in the face of his friend Jack who he'd always measured himself by. Jack had always looked and acted younger than his years. To see the man now drifting into old age unnerved Shelley. His time on this planet was drawing to an end. There was no longer any point running from this fact as every day his friend's ageing countenance would remind him.

To make matters worse, in the past ten years, Shelley had failed to save a penny of their winnings. Deep down he blamed Jack for this fecklessness. After all, wasn't it Jack who'd told him not to worry about cash? Colombia was going to be their big pay off! Jack had sworn blind and, as usual, Shelley had swallowed every word.

Still feeling low in spirits, he left the church. For twenty minutes after, he wandered aimlessly about the courtyard, chatting to the Colombian guards and watching the evening shadows as they crawled slowly across the dust at his feet. With every passing minute he knew a hard decision was to be made. As the sun finally set beyond the walls, with no decision made, he did what he'd always done while in Sevilla and stuck for answers. He sought the comfort and advice of Chantal.

~ ~ ~

"I still have options," Shelley muttered, more to himself than Chantal. Evening was drawing in and he was beginning to feel even more on edge. Greco's bus had long since gone and now he was beginning to regret not leaving.

"Of course."

"I know people in Costa Rica... San Jose."

"Good friends?" Chantal continued from her hammock. She wasn't looking at Shelley as she spoke. Her eyes were on the high ceiling, watching the mosquitoes as they flitted about the room's solitary light bulb. As she spoke, her left leg fell free from the hammock; a long, brown and slender limb, tanned to near perfection on the beaches of southern France. The tip of her small toes now touched the room's cold, stone floor. She began to push against the stone and as the hammock began to sway she spoke again, only this time louder, more insistent:

"Good friends?"

Shelley was standing outside, his elbows resting against the veranda's loose railings, his sixth cigarette that hour perched between hand and dry lip. Good friends? No. The people he knew in Costa Rica could not be described as friends. At best they were acquaintances. They were conmen: Nasty little creatures that made their livings convincing people to invest their cash with bogus stockbrokers. They operated from boiler rooms, sprinkled like painful sores all across San Jose. Nothing face to face. Their tricks were played out over the phone. They were actors, each and every one. Some of them were great. It had often occurred to Shelley that an honest career treading the boards would have suited them better.

"I don't have many friends left, only Jack really. I lost touch with the others."

"I find that very sad Sebastian," Chantal continued.

Shelley had noticed a gradual decrease in her affections toward him of late and the coolness of her reply only seemed to confirm the beginning of their end.

"I'm afraid friendship, like lovers, never quite convinced."

She ignored the dig, turning herself instead gently within the hammock. She now faced the room's whitewashed walls, already picking at its chipped plaster with her long fingernails.

"I can be in San Jose by the weekend."

"And Jack?"

"To hell with him," Shelley muttered under his breath. He didn't mean a word of it. Chantal knew it too and sensibly kept quiet.

The truth was, much to his shame, he'd never really done anything without Jack somehow involved. For as far back as he could remember, from their very first meeting as teenagers on the docks of Port Moresby, Jack had been the leader and Shelley his comfortable follower.

He smiled now, recalling their first meeting. 'Not to worry old son, it's a known fact that the tribes of Papua New Guinea are a peaceful bunch. Besides pygmies Shelley, pygmies...What danger could they pose?' Jack had lectured only minutes after introducing himself, having made a point of carrying Shelley's heavy luggage in their search for digs that night and knowing that such a kindly gesture would surely oblige Shelley to stay with him. 'New Guinea is simply brimming with gold my friend... Just waiting to be discovered!' Jack had continued, full of misplaced confidence. 'And did you know Shelley that Flynn himself lived here! Errol bloody Flynn! I tell you sir, this place is made for a pair of young swashbucklers like ourselves,' he'd rambled on very much excited.

Back then Jack had even possessed a passing resemblance for the young Australian actor. A fact not missed by Shelley or the many ladies that had subsequently filled his friend's insane life. Quite simply, Shelley had followed. Seduced by Jack's enthusiasm, his restlessness and inexhaustible lust for adventure he'd been unable to resist.

From the veranda Shelley eyed the lush green hills that rose high above the courtyard walls, themselves grey and dour in comparison. In appearance these hills were not a million miles away from those of New Guinea and it occurred to Shelley that Sevilla's picturesque mountain range would become the setting for his last adventure. Jack would never settle down. Shelley's remaining dream was to somehow make his bundle and then retire gracefully. Mexico appealed to him. He'd buy a large house near the ocean and spend the rest of his days leading a quiet and respectable life.

"What are you thinking Sebastian? What do you have?"

He felt Chantal's warm hands close about his waist a fraction before her soft voice whispered into his ear.

"We never did find any gold."

"Gold? What do you mean baby?"

"I was just a young lad fresh out of public school. The bloody fool knew it too," Shelley continued without explanation. 'I'd never stepped a foot outside England before. I suppose New Guinea had struck me as so exotic. The perfect cure for a life spent behind a bloody school desk."

"You sound so serious Sebastian."

"Well, I'm afraid we're in a serious situation Chantal."

"Oh, but you know I don't like it when you're in this frame of mind. You should try and be a little more like Jack. He doesn't take things so hard," she went on, squeezing him tighter, a shallow gesture that failed to convince either of them.

He'd leave Sevilla alone. Their relationship was drawing to a close and beside he saw too much of Jack whenever he looked into Chantal's wide, green eyes. She craved adventure too, perhaps her prime reason for traveling with them and not because of any overwhelming feeling for him. They'd met on the bus from Santa Marta to Bogota. Jack had been fast asleep when she'd taken the seat next to them. They'd been the only Europeans on the bus and yet they'd both kept their distance. Only when the driver of the bus had stopped for refreshments had Shelley ventured forward. Once outside, he'd bought her water and a pack of cigarettes. They'd talked for almost forty minutes while the other Colombian passengers had sat drinking tinto, chatting amongst themselves.

Chantal's conversation was the usual talk that travellers fell into: The countries she'd left behind, the strange people she'd met and places she'd yet to see. Her English was fluent too, at times spoken with only a hint of a French accent. She'd been wandering the globe for eight years, mostly teaching English.

"I hated Korea," she'd complained, her long back resting against the cafe wall, one of Shelley's cigarettes smoking away in her right hand.

"Such a sterile country. Very little imagination."

He had her age down at around forty-three, although she looked some years older. Too much caffeine, sun worship and nicotine abuse had aged her skin prematurely and the shabby looking clothes she wore did little to highlight what a very slender, feminine figure was, he suspected, beneath. She'd been teaching in Korea for five months when the school she'd been working for had gone bust. Her employers had failed to supply her with a correct working visa and she'd been forced to leave the country, still owed five thousand dollars.

Shelley remembered grinning as she'd relayed the tale. He'd spent time in Suwon with Jack and knew from experience that a lot of Korea's private academies were run by crooks.

"Did you try the French consulate? Always worth a shout," he'd poked.

"Five thousand dollars is a lot of cash to simply walk away from."

"I was a little scared to ask."

"Afraid?"

"You need a degree to teach in Korea. I bought mine in Thailand on the Khoa Sarn Road," she'd finished smiling. With that comment, Shelley had seen the potential for genuine friendship.

"You know, my friend and I are headed for a small town to the south of Bogota," he'd continued.

"You're more than welcome to join us if we take your fancy."

"Can I trust you?"

"Afraid not my dear. Are you willing to take the risk?"

Another broad smile and twelve miles into their new adventure Jack had snapped awake to find Shelley teaching Chantal the finer points to Texas hold 'em poker. Always the host, Jack had introduced a bottle of rum into the equation and quite soon their small bus had become a hotbed for amazing anecdotes, outrageous lies and impossible dreams. Inevitably, Jack had piped them to the post with his own tales but not without Chantal pushing them close.

She'd led an interesting life. Before Korea, she'd explored a great deal of South East Asia, drifting first from Thailand into Vietnam and from Vietnam to the Philippines. She'd settled for a time in Manila. Here she'd met and dated a middle-aged Canadian called Pete. Pete owned a string of girlie bars in downtown Makati and was kind enough to introduce Chantal into the fascinating world of Filipino investment banking.

"You worked in a boiler room too?" Jack had asked, genuinely impressed.

"Alabang Hills."

"Nice part of town," Shelley had added, recalling his time in Manila.

"Very nice... we had a five bedroom house, our own maids, and bodyguards ...everything!"

"But still you left," Jack had continued, already knowing why. Like himself, Chantal was a free spirit. Whatever comforts had been provided by her employers, they could never replace her need for independence.

"I felt trapped like in prison. They told me I couldn't leave the house alone under any circumstances. It was terrible! I think they were afraid I would talk to the other ex pats in town and blow their cover. So, I ran."

"A good move young lady," Jack had empathized.

"And where may I ask was your next destination?"

"I took a plane to Korea. I had friends in Seoul. They taught English. They put me in touch with a small academy on the outskirts of Suwon. But like

I said the school went bust and I lost a lot of money. So, I threw the dice and came here."

"Sounds like quite the adventure," Shelley added, happy to have met a kindred spirit.

"Any particular reason why you chose Colombia? There are a lot safer countries you could have gone too," Jack chipped away.

"South America is a big place!"

"It's cheap. I can still teach English if I choose, and..."

"And she's a little dangerous," Jack had interrupted with a knowing smile.

"Oui bien sûr...she's a little dangerous."

Convinced they were now singing from the same hymn sheet, Jack had begun to explain their own reasons for choosing Colombia. Shelley had kept a respectful silence throughout his speech, knowing that Jack's explanations were always far more entertaining than anything he could hope to conjure up. It took his friend a full thirty minutes to complete his sales pitch, during which time, inevitably, Chantal had been convinced. She'd follow them to Sevilla, if only for the free rum.

"Everything will work out fine Shelley. You must stop worrying like this," Chantal said now as she lay next to him in bed, her long, olive skinned arms again wrapped loosely about his midriff.

"Yes, I'm quite sure it will," he replied, unconvinced.

As he replied, Chantal slipped a delicate hand beneath her lover's thin cotton shirt where it began to slide contentedly across the warmth of his broad chest. Her long fingers soon discovered the slim silver necklace which hung loose about Shelley's thick neck and, like she always did, she began to toy with it gently between curious thumb and forefinger. After a time her fingers stopped moving and she fell into a light sleep, her hand still hidden beneath Shelley's thin cotton shirt.

Colombia wasn't all bad. With the day-to-day problems its citizens faced, Shelley had been humbled by the people's kindness and hospitality. He'd been taken aback too by the country's sheer beauty and he was pretty certain Jack felt the same way. In quiet moments he would often recall their first day in Bogota. Hopelessly lost and fatigued, he remembered with great clarity the kindly Colombian stranger who'd spent his entire morning, and the greater part of his afternoon, helping them find suitable lodgings. Indeed, most Colombians they'd encountered shared this same generosity of spirit.

Still, it wasn't long before Colombia's negatives were to rear their ugly head. Eight months previous, long before Raul and his compatriots had come to learn of their presence, when learning Spanish had seemed such a good idea, Shelley had begun to study the papers. In retrospect, it had been a bad idea. Every day, with each new article, reports of the paramilitaries and their random acts of cruelty against the civilian population were becoming more elaborate and even more shocking. In the end, he'd stopped reading them altogether. If the reporting reflected truthfully what was going on, then the rebels were inching closer to Sevilla every day. By early spring entire families were packing up and migrating to larger, less vulnerable cities.

Shelley had observed this exodus with a growing unease and had begun to question Jack's judgment in sticking put. It was around this time that Raul had discovered their presence, which had only added to their problems. Consequently, it quickly became too dangerous to leave the safety of the compound unless accompanied by a string of heavily armed bodyguards, or at the very least disguised in some fashion. By the time Samuel had appeared there was a general feeling amongst the locals that the rebels would invade Sevilla within days.

To make matters even more complicated, the family of one of their hostages had finally agreed to pay a large ransom, and Jack had become very reluctant to leave without having first collected it. Shelley had been tracking the family for weeks with phone calls and both parties had agreed on a middleman to broker the handover. The man's name was Church Rawlings. Church was to meet Shelley in person tomorrow afternoon to hand over a large payment in cash. In return, Jack would release their young American hostage, Joseph, and then everybody would be happy. The trouble was tomorrow evening was still many hours away and by then, Shelley was certain, Sevilla would have fallen to the rebels.

"Bugger it!" Shelley whispered, leaving the bed to grab his jacket. If Jack was too stubborn to listen to good reason then he'd take matters into his own hands. He'd fetch the cash himself. After all he knew the hotel where Rawlings was staying. He'd booked the fleapit himself not two days ago. Then he'd be away. Far away.

"Sebastian? Where are you going?"

"Across town to meet with Rawlings."

Hearing that name, Chantal lifted herself, half asleep, from the bed. Shelley had already opened the door. He'd turned its handle very gently hoping not to wake her, but the door's hinges were too old and too rusted to move silently. Chantal had always been a light sleeper; the lightest, and her inquisitive eyes had quickly snapped open.

"Across town alone? Are you crazy Sebastian? You'll be seen. Raul and his men will kill you for sure!"

"I'll take my chances."

"We should wait... Jack told us to wait."

"I'm afraid we no longer have that luxury."

As if reinforcing his words, far beyond the compound, beyond the hills and many villages that lived beneath their lush slopes, the crackle of distant gunfire entered the room.

"The paramilitaries will be on us within hours. Jack won't leave without his ransom cash and I can't let that happen," he continued, first snatching his revolver that lay across the bedside table and then rifling through its drawers to grab a handful of scattered bullets.

"And what about us? All you think about is Jack! Damn Jack this and damn Jack that!"

Shelley paused, one foot already outside.

"Us?" he eventually replied, stuffing a few of the bullets into the revolver's barrel. Chantal had already slipped on a baggy T-shirt. She sat at the bed's edge, the hem of her T-shirt riding just above her exposed knees.

"All you care about is Jack! You've always put him first!"

"Chantal, please..."

"If you die, what happens to me? Have you thought about that?"

Having snapped the barrel closed, Shelley again made to leave.

"What? Don't I even get a reply? You not man enough?"

"Like I said, friends and lovers, never quite convinced."

"And Jack?"

"Jack's the only family I have left. One day you might understand. Now, get some rest Chantal...And please, take some good advice when it's offered. Leave this town as soon as you can."

"Shelley. Wait!"

Ignoring her, he stepped outside, only stopping to close the door.

~ ~ ~

"Senor Locke, please Senor Locke, you must come quick!"

Samuel jolted upright in bed, finding a thick, unpleasant film of sweat now covering his body. Mario, Jack's young helper, stood over him, a hand still trying to shake the older man awake.

"Your Papa Senor Locke, please you must come quickly!" the boy continued, the panic in his voice even more evident. Samuel had just enough time to register Mario's presence before the boy had disappeared out the bedroom door.

"What the hell is going on?" he mumbled to himself, falling out of bed and into his clothes. Fairfax Hall had become a distant memory.

It was early afternoon now as Samuel stumbled, bleary eyed outside into the bright sunlight. A large, chattering group had formed in the courtyard's centre and as Mario's frantic words began to replay themselves, one particular word stuck in his mind – Papa.

Reaching the mob seconds later, Samuel pushed himself through their ranks to find his father slumped over the wounded body of Sebastian Shelley. The old Etonian had suffered quite a bad wound too. The poor sod grasped his stomach in what must have been absolute agony, and yet his trembling hands could do little to stem the massive flow of blood which now covered most of his lower torso and most of the cobblestones around him.

"Dad?"

Wearily, Jack glanced up at his son, a solitary tear running down the side of his face.

"They stabbed him! The bloody fools stabbed him!"

"Who? Who stabbed him?"

Before Jack could collect his thoughts and give a legible reply, Shelley, using whatever strength he had left, took firm hold of Jack's shirt and pulled him close. In response, Jack gently raised his friend's head to his ear.

"Yes Shelley?"

Shelley's mouth moved, tried to form the correct words, but could not quite manage the task. A series of low mumblings tumbled instead from his quivering lips and when the first trickles of blood began to follow Jack could no longer control himself. He began to weep.

Samuel felt suddenly helpless. He put a comforting arm around his father but the tears only increased. Soon after, Shelley's mouth stopped moving for good. For a short time there was silence, only broken by the occasional murmur from the surrounding crowd.

"He's gone dad," Samuel spoke softly, his arm still wrapped about his father's shoulders.

"I'm sorry."

"But he was my friend!"

Behind them, the crowd parted and two men stepped forward. Their names were Raffa and Saul, father and son.

"So, who go and fetch the money now Jack, hey?" Raffa was the first to speak. He was pushing fifty and when he spoke Samuel noticed that three of his bottom teeth were missing. Those that remained intact were nothing special either, chipped and discoloured. He was bald too except for those small tufts of grey hair which sprouted from behind his ears and the handful of long strands which ran across his forehead.

"Screw your bloody money you ugly swine! Shelley's dead!" Jack protested.

Arrogantly, Saul shrugged his heavy shoulders.

In thirty years' time, Samuel mused, the boy would come to look just like his father, only thinner, meaner looking.

"So what? He was running out on us, I did right to put a knife in his belly!" Saul said, spitting at the corpse as he finished.

Jack sprang to his feet like a man twenty years his junior and planted a beauty of a punch to the side of Saul's goblin face. The force of the punch threw the Colombian to the ground.

"Take that back! Take that bloody back!" Jack yelled, falling onto Saul and wrapping his hands about his scrawny neck.

"Dad!"

"Get off him Jack," Raffa shouted, trying to drag Jack off his son. The surrounding crowd, perhaps fearing a second death, began to edge away and it took Samuel's help to prize his father free.

"I'll rip his bleeding head off if he says anything like that again Raffa!" Jack screamed, both Raffa and Samuel now standing between him and a dazed looking Saul.

"Nobody is going to hurt anyone Jack...Okay?" Raffa replied, calmly. Jack tried to push his son to one side, but Samuel just about held his ground.

"Jack?"

"Just keep your son quiet Raffa...You understand that?"

"He will not say one more bad word...Saul?"

Slowly, Saul climbed to his feet. He still looked dazed, surprised by the power in the older man's punch, and now boasted a blooded lip for the revelation.

"Saul?"

"Sure, I keep quiet, but tell me this, why your good friend try to sneak away? You tell me that Senor Locke."

Jack paused. They'd already agreed to collect the cash later that evening and Shelley had known already how dangerous it was for him to walk around town alone.

"He would not have run out on us!" Jack replied, convinced there had to be some other explanation. Saul shook his head.

"We all agreed a pick-up time. We had men ready to watch over him. He went too early! He was going to take the cash for himself!"

Again, Jack made a lunge for Saul. Again, Raffa and Samuel held him back.

"I thought I warned you before. He'd never run out on me! Now keep that mouth of yours shut!"

"You can't blame our men for feeling anger Jack. You promised them money. So far we see nothing!" Raffa continued.

"Are you bloody deaf? Have you not been listening? Shelley would have had your cash later tonight! Your intelligent son has just buggered that plan up!"

"If they want their loot that bad, why can't they fetch it themselves?" Samuel inquired, turning to look directly into Raffa's wide brown eyes. The Colombian smiled. Jack almost managed a chuckle too.

"For the same reason these bleeders stick to me like glue. It all comes down to trust dear boy. Trust. Do you think I'd let one of these buggers fetch all that cash on their lonesome? Not a chance. He'd be in Rio before nightfall. I'm afraid Shelley was the only decent soul amongst us!"

"Then why not send your own son?" Raffa continued.

"You could trust your own son couldn't you, Jack?"

"Don't push your luck Raffa...I'll put you on the floor next."

Saul stepped forward, his meaty fists tightly clenched.

"I'm serious Jack, who else is there? Only you and Shelley knew the pick-up location. So why not tell Samuel? We even send a couple of men to escort him."

"Yes, I bet you bloody would too."

"Ah, come on Jack, you have to learn to trust somebody one day," Raffa continued, a huge grin now visible across his face.

"He's right Dad, I'll go."

"Be quiet!"

"Listen to your son Jack. It's the only solution left."

"Dad?"

"I said be quiet!"

"Time's running out old friend. Your men are restless. They cannot wait much longer. They have families to feed also. A son would not run out on his father."

Deep in thought, Jack slowly turned to face Samuel.

"You sure you can do this? I mean dead certain?"

"Don't worry; I can take good care of myself. I had a rough time as a kid, remember?"

"Don't get smart, this really isn't the time for it."

"Then just tell me where I have to go. I'll bring you back the cash, no problem."

"Well?" Raffa pushed, victory in sight.

For a second, Jack buried his head into his hands.

"I just lost a dear friend. Do you think I could bear to lose a son as well?" he finally replied, first glancing over toward Shelley's body, and then facing Samuel once more.

"I can do this Dad..."

Shaking his head, Jack took a couple of strides forward.

"I hope you bloody can..."

Leaning forward, Jack whispered something into his son's ear. Samuel nodded intently.

"You tell him?" Raffa inquired, looking more than a little uncertain.

"Don't worry, I told him."

"Then what are we waiting for?"

"Don't panic, we have hours left," Jack retorted, glancing back toward Samuel. For a second time he began to whisper:

"Shelley was to meet Rawlings at two dead on. By my watch that gives you three hours. Find a bar, any bar, and keep your bloody head out of sight. You got that?"

"I'll be okay."

Reluctantly, Jack smiled.

"Samuel!"

"Yeah?"

"You'd best take this along. Just in case."

From inside his trouser belt, Jack handed his son a pistol.

"Cheers, but I'm sure I'll be fine," Samuel replied, stuffing the gun into his own belt.

"We could have a couple of men go with him Jack, make sure he is okay."

"No thanks Raffa, my boy will be fine on his own," Jack replied, unconvinced. "I wouldn't want your boys getting any fancy ideas with all that loot and nobody to share it with!"

Raffa smiled. Jack was moving to tend to Shelley's body once again, when, from inside Sebastian's room, one of the Colombian guards stumbled out, a shaking hand plastered across his pale face.

"Senor! Senor Locke!"

As the guard spoke, Saul slowly began to edge away.

"Oh, heavens! What is it now?" Jack replied.

"The girl Senor Locke. Shelley's girl. She dead too!"

~ ~ ~

Church Rawlings was getting mighty concerned. It was two, dead on. He'd jumped when the clock tower had first struck the hour, and now he wondered how much longer he'd have to wait. He was halfway through his third cup of black coffee and still there was no sign of his elusive contact. What name had they given this elusive contact? Shelley? Sebastian Shelley. Damn silly name. No sign of him.

Taking a long sip from his cup, his big, froglike, green eyes peeking just over its chipped, dirtied rim, he scanned the central square searching for a small, plump Englishman who might look like he would answer to the name of Shelley. To his growing frustration, he could find no one remotely close. The people who streamed past him were mostly Colombian locals.

There were a few who might have been European, but none of them fitted the description of the guy he'd been given. He didn't want to sit around all day either waiting for this guy to show up, despite what the Walker family were paying him. At that moment in time he had roughly one hundred thousand dollars tucked away in a battered old suitcase beneath his chair and Sevilla didn't look like the sort of town where a fella should be carrying around a battered old suitcase packed full of used notes.

He was pulling out his mobile and punching in the contact number when a crisp voice sounded off to his right.

"Mr. Church Rawlings?"

Church glanced up. This guy didn't look like a Shelley. He was English alright, but too tall, too young.

"Yeah?"

"I'm a friend of young Joseph, I think we have something to discuss?"

"You don't look like the fella they described."

"The guy they described is dead Mr. Rawlings," Samuel coolly replied, taking a seat opposite the large, middle-aged American who stood out a mile. The tacky Hawaiian shirt and his bronzed, bald head seemed to do it. Church's jaw was still hanging loose when Samuel slapped the pistol onto the table.

"You have our money, Mr. Rawlings? I really hope you have our money."

"Now listen up pup, there ain't any need for that, I have the cash, just take it easy." A gang of filthy looking street kids, having spotted the two, choice foreigners chatting, now decided to put their charms to the test and idled over. Samuel's hand reached for the gun once more.

"We don't have all day Mr. Rawlings."

"Sure kid, I understand, but nobody told me about you, you've got to see things from my position."

"Chucky, If you don't show me that cash right away, I'm going to stick a hole in you where really there shouldn't be one, do you understand that?" Samuel replied, trying to look as menacing as possible and really quite enjoying the role. Church twitched. For a few seconds his entire body seemed to twitch.

"Now look, kid..."

Samuel cocked the trigger. A tingle of excitement ran through him as he did and he couldn't hide a wry smile.

"Mr. Rawlings..."

At that precise moment, the gang of street kids, unperturbed by the presence of a gun, especially one that was now pointing at somebody else's head, bounded over.

"Hey! Americano! Plata! Plata!" they all began to scream in tandem, grabbing at both men's shirt sleeves.

"Get lost!" Samuel snapped, holding the gun as steady as he could under the new barrage.

"Yeah, do what the nice man wants kids and beat it!"

"Well? I'm waiting Mr. Rawlings."

Doing his best to ignore the gang of pests, Church slowly reached under his table and pulled out the stuffed suitcase.

"Well, there you go young man, every last dollar."

"Open it."

"Here?"

"I said open it!" Samuel repeated, inching the gun closer toward Church's sweaty forehead. Even the kids took a collective step back. Reluctantly, Church opened the case. Samuel waved the gun quickly toward the kids and all their thoughts of a better future vanished.

"It's all there Mr..."

"Locke, Mr. Locke."

"Every last dollar, counted it out myself. The Walker family just want their Joseph back safe."

"Of course they do," Samuel continued, carefully closing the case and standing back up.

"Is that it? Can I go now?" Church asked, nervously wiping away sweat from his forehead with what looked like a very used handkerchief.

"You can go now Mr. Rawlings."

"And what about Joseph? What about the boy?"

"I guess little Joe gets to be released, just as soon as we've counted this lot out properly you understand," Samuel replied, tapping the case.

"But when will I hear from you?" Church asked. Samuel didn't know. He hadn't thought that far ahead.

"Later on tonight Mr. Rawlings, later on tonight," he eventually replied, leaving the table and heading back across the square.

11

Payback

Raul considered himself the king of spin. He was a shocking liar, and when he told his lies, people tended to believe them. There were no rebels about to attack Sevilla. With a little help from Leopold, he'd started that rumour himself many weeks ago; a very clever, calculated move. The locals in town all knew of his links with the rebel army, and as soon as their rumours had begun to circulate around town, the vast majority of its people had been beating themselves up to be nice to him.

As with all lies, the very best lies were often based on some truth. To the far south of Colombia the rebels were indeed ordering mayors to leave towns and executing those who stayed. But Sevilla, being that further north, would be safe for the time being. It was all just a question of how long he could keep the lie bubbling over.

Raul ran a very careful finger along the rack of baseball bats. Part of the pleasure, a good deal of the pleasure came from those lingering moments of anticipation before the beatings actually began, and were only surpassed when the screaming started and those looks of agony set in. That was when the fun would really start.

Still studying the rack of baseball bats, Raul spoke:

"Hold him still Leopold...He needs to be still."

Leopold gave the drug mule a swift punch to the belly. The poor man would have groaned, except for the gag which had been stuffed deep into his mouth. The gag would only be removed as and when the punishment began.

"Are you holding him steady?"

"He's steady Raul, real steady."

"Good."

The small Colombian farmer lay flat on his back across Raul's office table, both his legs and arms having been strapped down. Leopold stood peering into the man's terrified face, smiling to himself. Before he'd met Raul, he never would have thought he'd owned such a cruel, sadistic streak, but over a period of months he'd come to enjoy the feeling of power it gave him to watch, and to be in part responsible for another man's suffering. It was a road that once taken could not be left easily, and like with any addiction, the form of torture would have to be reinvented each time in order to maintain the same level of buzz.

Leopold punched the farmer's stomach once more, this time harder, adding to his own pleasure.

"That's enough Leopold, take out his gag," Raul ordered, now standing over the farmer, a huge carving knife in his right hand. Leopold quickly removed the gag.

"Senor! Por favor!"

"Quiet!" Leopold snapped, slapping the prisoner across the face. Again, the farmer fell silent, his feeble body shaking,

"You know something Leopold, you just can't get the mules these days!" Raul continued, watching Leopold as he now ripped open the man's shirt.

"I hear you boss."

"You give a peasant the opportunity to make some cash, feed his family, and what happens? His bottle goes!"

"Well, what can you do?" Leopold spoke. He was getting excited. His favourite part was coming.

"I'm not going to wait for nature to take its course, I know that much."

"I don't follow you Raul."

Raul grinned, first raising the blade level with his own shoulder and then plunging it deep into the Colombian's exposed belly. The man almost formed a scream, but the shock of what had just taken place, caused his entire body to freeze.

"Jesus Raul!"

Expertly, Raul sliced open the man's lower torso. The farmer's guts then tumbled out onto the table like heated popcorn, followed by copious amounts of blood. Usually this sort of thing would have made quite a mess of the office, but having learnt from a great deal of experience, Raul had pinned several large, plastic sheets across both the floor and walls.

Although still alive, the farmer had long since passed out. Raul slipped on a thick pair of rubber gloves and rammed his fist down hard into the man's open belly. After some seconds of fumbling, he removed his hand that now grasped two small, plastic bags of cocaine.

"Good work boss," Leopold complimented, inwardly upset that it had all come to an end so quickly.

"Now we find somebody else to do the job," Raul went on, slapping the two dripping bags onto his desk, casually removing the gloves.

Maria was on her hands and knees, busy wiping down the stage. She occasionally looked up from her work and cast a curious eye over toward Raul's office. It had been closed for some time now and she'd begun to wonder what could possibly be going on inside. In just over one hour from now the first of that evening's punters would be stepping through the door. It sickened her even to think of them. She'd have to be nice; all smiles if she even hoped to make any decent cash and this made her even more depressed.

She'd select a drunk. The drunks were by far the easiest to manipulate. She could rip them off and then complain to the bouncers if they started to act up. Sometimes, even if they were innocent, she would lie to the bouncers and get the pigs beaten. It made her feel a little better at least.

"Maria!" Maria looked up to find Samuel standing by the stage, all smiles.

"Samuel! What the hell are you doing here?"

"Is that your best welcome?"

She glanced nervously back toward Raul's office and then quickly crawled to the edge of the stage; cleaning cloth still in hand.

"You will get us both killed!"

"Not if you come with me, right now," he replied, raising the battered suitcase.

"Look, I bought cash too, plenty of cash!"

Maria's expression softened.

"Where were you last night? I waited and waited, you never show!"

"I'll explain things later. First, we gotta go Maria!"

"Samuel, Raul is in his office right now, one word from me and he'll rip off your stupid head!"

Samuel smiled. "I don't think you'd do that...I think you like me too much."

"Oh, really?"

"Yes, really."

Maria threw the cloth to the stage.

"Samuel, you are a sweet guy but..."

Samuel dropped the suitcase and kissed Maria full on the lips.

"Samuel!"

"Well, you have a choice. Are you coming with me? Or do I leave this flea pit alone?"

She hesitated. She was ready to answer when the office door flew open. Raul and Leopold stepped out. Spotting them, she leapt from the stage and quickly dragged Samuel into one of the smaller rooms where a private dance could be paid for. Once inside, she pinned him against the back wall.

"Do I take this as being a yes?"

"Be quiet," she replied, slapping a hand across his mouth. Raul was now pacing the stage perimeter, wondering where Maria had gone.

"Please don't see us, please don't see," she whispered, her hand still clasped over Samuel's mouth. Raul turned momentarily from the stage, his eyes immediately fixing on the smaller room. Maria was still pressed up against Samuel's body as both parties locked eyes.

"I think we're in trouble," Samuel then whispered into her ear. Having navigated the stage, Raul now walked calmly toward the smaller room. Very gently, Samuel began to pull the pistol from his belt.

"Hold it right there," he warned as Raul entered, slowly raising the gun until it was pointing at the Colombian's head.

"Who is this Maria?"

"My name is Samuel, Samuel Locke...And this young lady is coming with me."

"Samuel Locke?" Raul repeated.

"Didn't you hear me the first time?"

"Then you are the son of Jack Locke, Si?"

"This really is a small town."

"You are the son of Jack Locke?" Maria now spoke, genuinely surprised.

"Don't tell me you know him too?"

"Enough! The girl stays here," Raul interrupted.

"Screw you!"

"You heard the girl," Samuel added, taking hold of Maria's hand and slowly beginning to edge them both out the smaller room. Having reached the main stage, Leopold took up a safe position behind his boss, almost falling to his knees in his eagerness to be out of range.

"Leopold, you disgust me."

"I'm sorry Raul."

"You're going to pay for this Samuel," Raul continued, Leopold still cowering behind him.

"I'm going to make you both suffer," he finished, watching as they then slipped quietly out the club.

"Leopold?"

"Yes Raul."

"Go fetch the shotguns."

"Yes boss."

Leopold jumped to his feet and raced for the office. Raul remained where he was, his eyes fixed on the door, through the door, with vivid images of Samuel covered in bullet holes. He didn't even notice the battered old suitcase which leant against the stage, and would not have given it much attention even if he had. His mind was elsewhere; his objective clear.

"I'm going to make them pay for this."

"Where are we going?" Maria questioned, already half way across the town square. She was smiling as she ran, perhaps the first time she'd felt happy in a long while.

Samuel held her hand tightly, and she could feel her fingers turning numb as he dragged her along. Still, she didn't care. She was away from Raul and that was the most important thing. As they ran, she glanced up at Samuel. His eyes were fixed straight ahead and hardly noticed her attention. Maybe, she thought, just maybe, they could share some sort of future together. The idea both excited and depressed her; they were still in a great deal of danger.

"Samuel? Where are we running to?"

Suddenly, he stopped. It was late evening. Only a handful of town locals loitered about the square and each of them to a man now missed the look of absolute horror which had planted itself across Samuel's face.

"Samuel? What is wrong?"

"The suitcase."

"The what?" Maria repeated, annoyed that his thoughts could be considering something else other than their blossoming relationship.

"The bloody suitcase!" he snapped back, letting go of her hand and sprinting back toward the strip club.

"Samuel!"

For a second, he half turned.

"Keep going, find the convent."

"I no hear you!"

"The Convento del Santo, tell them you're a friend, tell them anything, just make sure they let you in, okay?" he shouted.

"I won't be long."

He turned sharply, and Maria watched as he bolted for the strip club, his tall frame growing smaller as each long stride took him closer toward the building. He was nearing the main doors as they burst open; Raul and Leopold spilling out.

For one terrifying moment, Maria feared Raul would see Samuel, but Samuel, in the very nick of time, had managed to duck into a side alley, just as the doors had flown open.

Both men now jogged into the square. Raul immediately spotted Maria and gave chase. Watching him sprint toward her, she hesitated, before spinning herself around, determined to find the convent.

Jack could not recall the last time he'd discussed religion, certainly not with Shelley. To both men religion had always existed in direct conflict with how they'd chosen to lead their lives, and so had been generally ignored.

They'd both held values of course, certain codes of conduct but nothing ever set in stone. Better to live, and sin; and then repent those sins a few hours before the big heave-ho than to live a lifetime with one eye forever on the rule-book, with very little chance of ever coming up to scratch. It had made perfect sense to Jack.

Had Shelley even bothered to see a priest recently? The very idea made him shudder. It would have been a long chat if he had. Now his best friend was dead and he felt terribly guilty. To make matters worse, the Colombians had put a bullet through Chantal too and thrown both their bodies to the flames. Life was cheap in South America.

Standing at a distance, Jack watched as a further bundle of logs was hurled onto the bonfire. Shelley's diminutive body had almost completely dissolved now. Jack could make out tiny bits of charred corpse through the flickering flames, but very little else. Had Shelley even wanted to be cremated? Christ, there was such an awful lot about his friend that he hadn't known.

More logs were added. The fire roared. Black smoke began to billow out by the bucket load, and the gathering crowds were forced to take tentative steps back. Jack took a swig from a half empty bottle of wine, watching Shelley's remaining ashes gently float skyward, where a faint breeze then caught hold and blew them up toward the courtyard wall and over. Such a nice way to go, Jack thought, screwing the cork back into the bottle.

"Hey, Jack, you come up here, pronto!"

Jack's bloodshot eyes returned to the wall. One of the men who stood guard was waving down at him.

"What is it for heaven's sake?" Jack replied, not wanting to climb all the way up to meet him just to answer another question that would involve the non-payment of wages.

"It's a girl Jack."

"Girl?" Jack mumbled.

"What bloody girl?"

The Colombian shrugged.

"She say she know you."

"Oh, for God's sake!"

Letting the bottle of wine smash to the ground, there were plenty of others left in stock, Jack stomped angrily toward the courtyard wall.

"Which bloody girl knows me?" he continued to grumble as he climbed the unsteady ladder that would lead him to the wall's summit.

"I said what bloody girl?"

The bemused looking guard pointed nervously down into the square. Jack found the hysterical young lady now banging her tiny fists against the courtyard doors.

"Can we help you at all?"

The girl's head shot up.

"Let me in! You must let me in!"

"Will you please stop banging our door like that. I have the most terrible headache!"

Maria did as he asked.

"Now who on earth are you?" Jack continued.

"I know Samuel, I his friend...Let me in!" she wailed, again banging the door, this time with even more vigour. Curious, both Raffa and Saul had joined the group.

"Who is this?" Raffa asked. The girl looked familiar, but he couldn't think from where.

"Jack, who is she?"

"Let her in," Jack replied softly, his voice suddenly calm, serious.

"But who is she?"

"I said let her bloody in damn it!" Jack thundered, his face turning bright red with sudden rage. Raffa could only assume that Jack knew the girl and so called down to the men in the courtyard.

"Okay, do what he say, open the gates."

The courtyard gates were unlocked. Maria could not wait for them to open fully, and so squirmed her way through the earliest crack. Once inside, she collapsed into the dust, exhausted.

"Get her some water!" Jack ordered from the top of the ladder, going as fast as he could to reach the bottom. It wasn't easy. His knees had been playing him up for years and now they ached something rotten as he made his way slowly, very carefully, down the steep ladder.

Skipping from the bottom rung, a wooden bowl of water was then handed to him. Gently cradling the girl's head in his arm, he placed the bowl beneath her dry lips.

"Here, take a few sips, there's no rush. Nice and easy," he finished, waving the gathered crowd of men back.

"That's it my dear, nice and easy."

"Gracias."

"I don't think we've had the pleasure."

Maria looked up at him, her expression blank.

"What is your name dear?"

"Maria."

"Maria," Jack repeated. He was sure he'd seen her face somewhere around town, but was equally certain they had never spoken before.

"And you are Jack, Si?"

"Jack Locke, that's right, how did you know my name?"

"Your son, Samuel, he tell me about you."

"That's right; you mentioned his name, is he alright?"

She fell silent. She went to take another sip but Jack pulled the bowl away.

"Maria? Is my son alright?"

"He go back to the club."

"Club?"

"To fetch something, a bag I think he say."

"A suitcase perhaps, he went back for a suitcase, Si?"

"Si, si that was it."

As a reward, Jack let her sip from the bowl.

"And where is he now Maria? Is he safe?"

Again she hesitated.

"I think a man named Raul could be after him," she eventually replied. Jack handed her the bowl. His thoughts began to whirl. He knew the man she spoke of and had come to fear him during the months he'd been holed up in Sevilla. The rumours were he held strong links with the rebel army and that didn't bode well for Samuel or any of them.

"Why? How did Raul get mixed up in all this mess?"

Maria shrugged but Jack could see in her eyes that she was holding something back.

"I need to know everything Maria. If you want me to help Samuel then I need to have all the facts at hand."

"I like Samuel, he like me too, we become very close, you understand?"

"And what is your point Maria? What has this got to do with Raul?" Jack continued. Maria bowed her head as he spoke and watching her, a feeling of complete dread began to cloud his mind. His next words were spoken very softly:

"Please don't tell me you're his girlfriend Maria? Please don't tell me that."

"Raul is a pig! I hate him!"

"Maria, are you Raul's girlfriend?" Jack persisted. She didn't reply, but then she really didn't have to. The look of guilt her faced now displayed was confession enough. Jack stood. Of all the stupid things to do. His own son was now fooling with the one girl in town whose boyfriend really could bring the rebels crashing down on top of them all if he so chose.

"Will Samuel be okay?" Maria asked timidly, clutching the bowl to her chest. Jack ignored her. He hadn't the energy to lie. He went to reach for his pistol but then remembered it was with Samuel.

"Jack!" a loud voice from above suddenly called out. Jack found the courtyard wall. This time it was Raffa who was calling his name.

"What is it now?"

"Somebody outside wants to speak with you."

"Samuel? Is Samuel back?"

With the mere mention of his name, Maria had jumped to her feet.

"No Jack, it is Raul, Raul wishes to speak with you," Raffa replied.

~ ~ ~

For some time Raul had followed Maria across the square, toward the convent gates. He'd watched the gates slowly open and Maria disappear inside. Samuel was nowhere to be seen and Raul could only assume that he'd reached the relative safety of the convent first, having left Maria to fend for herself.

There was a small water fountain not far from the main gates and now Raul leant his burly frame against its smooth, white stone. Leopold, forever unfit, simply crashed out across the dirt. His boss could do all the talking. He'd had enough for one day.

Both men had been waiting for perhaps five minutes when Raul had spotted Raffa appearing briefly from behind one of the courtyard wall's turrets. Quickly, he'd called out to him, given voice to his demands, and, to his mild surprise, found himself facing Jack Locke within a matter of minutes. All you had to do is ask.

He'd known about Jack for many months, had even come to admire the man's chutzpah. Sevilla was a small town. For most of the year they were in direct competition, but Raul had managed to turn a blind eye to this. Why not? There were always plenty of foreign backpackers to choose from, and as long as the man remembered to keep his operation discreet, he'd not seen a problem. Up until now. Now the situation had changed.

Jack's son had crossed a line. The boy had made a pass at his girl, perhaps even worse, and now his pride was at stake. Jack, framed between two turrets, was the first to speak:

"What do you want Raul?"

Raul dipped his hand lightly into the water fountain. He didn't drink, but instead wiped both his brow and neck. He was a man who liked to be in control. He wasn't going to let Jack rush him. He alone would set the pace of this conversation.

"I don't have all day Raul," Jack continued, beginning to lose his patience. He wasn't afraid of Raul. He knew Raul had links, dangerous links, but over the years he'd stood up to far better opposition. He thought of Bethnal Green and all those colourful characters that he and Shelley had put in their place. Who was this pup trying to intimidate? The bloody cheek!

"Well?"

Raul stood himself tall, his full six five; shoulders back, chest puffed out. He was not a man with whom you picked a fight lightly.

"You have the girl with you?"

"Yes, Maria is here, is she a friend of yours?" Jack answered. Raul grinned. He'd have to be careful around this man. It would be easy to end up liking him.

"I'd very much like to see her, if that is okay Senor Locke?"

"Now, that is a shame because I don't think Maria wishes to see you right now. I believe Maria would feel far happier if you were to just toddle off!"

Raul took a few moments to compose himself. Then again, he mused, it could be easier to hate this guy.

"You have a son Senor Locke?"

Jack paused. Apart from the other chap who sat slumped next to the water fountain, there was no sign of Samuel. Either he was already dead or had managed to escape Raul's clutches. Whatever the truth, Jack realized he'd still have to play it dumb. If Samuel was wandering around town, the suitcase full of cash in tow, then it was far better that Raul remained in the dark.

"What about him?"

"I caught your son with my girl Jack, and I have to say, I'm not a happy man."

As Raul finished speaking, Jack glanced back into the courtyard. He could see Maria seated near one of the convent rooms, a couple of his men doing their best to calm her down. She was still in tears and didn't look like stopping for quite some time.

"You caught my son with your girlfriend, have I got that right Raul?"

"Maria means everything to me Senor Locke, I hope you understand?"

Jack closed his eyes and for a brief moment ground his teeth. The bloody idiot! He'd kill Samuel himself once he got his hands on him. Raul continued:

"You and I are the same I think. We come to Sevilla to make some cash. We chose the same method of going about this and it was okay. There is plenty to go around and I didn't mind sharing. But now Jack, now your son has embarrassed me, hurt me deeply, and I can't just let that go."

"Well, what is it that you want Raul?"

"Your son and the girl Jack, hand them both over and I will let you live. It simple, si?"

Just as Jack's brain began to spin out of control in its search for a reply that would cover all bases, he spotted something which offered it immediate relief. His eyes fixed on the town square. Here, a nervous looking figure now edged its way very carefully past the houses, a large, battered suitcase in one hand, a tiny, black pistol in the other. Samuel was safe after all. Jack grinned.

"No!" he then replied.

"Que?" Raul continued, this time removing one hand from his trouser pocket in order to shield his tender eyes from the sun, almost as if being able to see Jack clearly would somehow alter his previous rebuttal.

"I said no," Jack repeated with more confidence, beginning to enjoy this little game.

"I don't think you understood what I said Senor Locke, If you don't hand them over, I will have to kill you all, and I have the right friends to do the job Jack," Raul rattled on, his own confidence clearly shaken. If Jack was bluffing then he was very good at it. Even Leopold, who'd so far decided to opt out of all negotiation, now sat himself upright against the water fountain, genuinely surprised with Jack's new line.

Jack didn't doubt Raul's words for one second. But if Samuel could reach them with the cash maybe later on that evening, he could pay off his men and be out of town long before the first rebel soldier stepped foot inside Sevilla. At least Shelley would be smiling to himself, wherever he was at that point in time.

"Do what you please Raul. Samuel and the girl stay here and that sir is my final answer," Jack finished, very pleased indeed.

For the moment Samuel was safe. He still had the suitcase, and if he was half as clever as his old man, then he would find a way back into the convent. Raul could go screw himself. Indeed Raul now looked blankly at Leopold who could only shrug.

"I'm not bluffing Senor!"

"I've heard all I've needed to hear thanks very much."

"Then fine! Tomorrow morning you will find others waiting for you, others far less reasonable than I Jack Locke! I think you know who I mean."

Jack knew alright. He meant the FARC paramilitaries. He just had to hope that Samuel didn't screw up.

"You must do what you think is best Raul," Jack shouted back, hoping his own show of bravado wouldn't cause him to fall flat on his face. Both frustrated and impressed, Raul gave Leopold a swift kick to the stomach, and once he was stood, both men made their way back to the club.

Samuel slid quickly back into the alleyway as he watched Raul and Leopold slither past. He pressed the suitcase tight to his chest and prayed that neither man would turn and catch sight of him. They didn't. Both continued across the square, heads down, without once looking up. He hugged the case even closer as they disappeared from view. He was beginning to feel the true weight of his responsibility. In his arms he carried with him not only his own future, but also the future of all those other people who were now waiting for him back inside the convent, especially those poor sods who were kept huddled up out of sight in the cellars.

He wasn't sure exactly how much was in the case, but he suspected quite a lot. It felt so heavy in his embrace, and as these thoughts continued to circle his mind, the temptation to just flee became stronger. What had his father ever done for him? At that very moment he could make for Bogota and quite rightly feel no remorse. He could take the money and call it compensation for all those long, childhood years of neglect.

Samuel closed his eyes and tried to think clearly. Raul and Leopold could return at any given moment. The choice was clear. Jack Locke or scarper with all the loot. For perhaps the first time in his adult life he had a real notion as to what it might be like to live as Jack Locke had lived. He shuddered. The idea both excited and repulsed him.

12

Last Stand

"The only one I ever really trusted," Jack confided in the dog who lay curled up by his side. The old Labrador retriever was both deaf and blind in one eye. His name was Rio, and he often sat next to Jack who liked to stroke his delicate ears and reminisce about the good old days. Rio was the best listener in town. He never challenged Jack's version of the past and always seemed grateful to be in his company. They sat together, as they did most evenings; their eyes on the bonfire, watching its dying embers fizzle out.

"Shelley was a good stick Rio, but you can never really trust anyone, not really," Jack rambled on, doing his very best impression of a pub bore. If Rio had been human and of sound hearing, he would have got up and made his excuses a long time ago. As it was, he remained with Jack, enjoying the familiar hand which gently ran down his spine. Jack missed Shelley something rotten. By nature Jack was a sentimental man and all evening his thoughts had been torn between Samuel's safe return, the cash, Shelley's untimely death, the rebels and his previous life back in London. More often than not, in times of great stress, Jack's thoughts would return to the old East End, his childhood home, and the place where he'd spent much of his early adult life.

The great East End, where criminal gangs had built their empires long before the police had come to understand the term organized crime. He'd been there at its very beginnings, at the very hub of things. He thought of his old pub back in Bethnal Green. He thought too of all the other seedy drinking holes, gambling dens and billiard halls he'd once known and loved. The good old East End – hardened drinkers, boxing enthusiasts, brothels and all the stolen goods you could lay your hands on. He missed it all. Of course by now London would have changed beyond all recognition, at least for Jack. New gangs were now taking over his capital: Yardies, Albanians, Kosovans. It was one other reason why he'd stayed put in South America for so long. He was afraid of what reality might throw at him if ever he were to return. South America had nothing on London, or his memories.

"I think I keep you company," Maria spoke, taking a seat on the log next to Jack.

"Are you okay," she continued. She'd been watching Jack for quite some time. Despite the dog, he'd looked so alone, so lost in thought, she'd simply felt compelled to sit with him.

"Try and stay young if you can girl, never grow old, never grow old."

"I don't think you look so old Jack."

"Well don't let my doctor hear you say that, he'd have a fit!"

As he replied, she wrapped her arm under his.

"What is his name?" she questioned, glancing down at Rio who'd already drifted off to sleep.

"I'm not too sure, he never speaks to me."

She smiled and hugged Jack's arm even tighter.

"His name is Rio. I found him wandering the streets of that city many years ago. He was just a pup. A lost pup with nowhere to go. I took pity on him and he's been with me ever since."

"That's nice."

"And what's more, during all those years, I've not heard a single word of complaint, not one! You know, I find that sort of loyalty amazing!"

Maria listened quietly. During their brief acquaintance, she'd come to enjoy Jack's company; the effortless way he told stories, his ease at making everything sound so very funny and plausible, even when it was the most outrageous lie. He made her feel safe, and yet despite this, his jovial attitude had begun to irritate her somewhat.

She knew it was all done for her benefit, Jack's special way of keeping up her spirits, but Samuel was still missing and no amount of silly jokes would bring him back. For just a moment then, Maria wanted Jack to be serious.

"You think Samuel will be okay?"

Jack paused, his hand returning to the dog's thick, mostly matted coat.

"I told you already, Samuel will be fine, just fine," he eventually replied.

"Then I would like to talk...A serious talk Jack."

"About what?" he continued, his face already beginning to tense as she spoke. He had an idea what was coming next and just knew he wasn't going to like it.

"About the past, about Samuel."

Jack didn't like to talk about the past, not where Samuel and Catherine were concerned. He didn't have many regrets, he didn't believe in regrets, but if there was one, then it would be leaving Catherine and the boy behind. She'd never stood for any of his nonsense, even in his blackest of moods, when his volcanic temper erupted; she'd never allowed herself to be intimidated. Catherine was the first woman that he'd ever truly respected. Certainly she was a better human being than him.

"I first met Samuel's mother when she was a student. She was at Oxford, studying law. Her family was all very well to do. You can imagine their horror when they learnt about me Maria, we didn't even tell them about the baby until after his birth. Not that it made any difference. When they found out, they told Catherine to have the child adopted. They told her that she'd never see a penny of her inheritance if she stayed with me. She was nineteen, her whole life ahead of her..."

"So you left?"

"Eventually, yes, I left."

"But Catherine, what did she want? She say she want you to go?"

"The past is past Maria, what's done is done, can't we talk about something different?"

"I think this girl loved you Jack."

"I suppose, I suppose I loved her too."

Maria pulled her arm free from under Jack's and took hold of his hand.

"Samuel is still very angry, but if you just talk to him, I know you could be friends."

"You really think he'd listen? I get the impression he's past caring."

"I know your son for only a short time but I feel he just wants answers; he just doesn't know how to ask."

Jack knew she was right and smiled.

"You know, you're a fine one to be talking about my son's well-being. You have a very dangerous boyfriend who would like nothing more than to see both of us dead."

She lowered her head. He'd expected some kind of protest but none came. If it was a deep and meaningful she was after then perhaps now would be the right time for him to ask a few questions of his own. This girl had come out of nowhere and it bothered him. It bothered him a great deal.

"This isn't some sort of game is it Maria? I'd hate to think that it was," he continued, having decided to push the matter a little harder. Sometimes it was the only way to get at the truth.

"What do you mean by that?" she replied, her eyes suddenly wide; startled. He paused, softened his voice.

"Raul is your boyfriend; perhaps you were feeling taken for granted. Decided to make him jealous? Very convenient that Samuel came around when he did."

Maria pulled her hand away and Jack could see that she'd been deeply hurt by his words.

"Perhaps you even see my son as an easy way out of town. I wouldn't blame you Maria, I can imagine how a man like Raul would treat a girl like you, but I don't want to see Samuel messed about."

He thought she would leave at that point, he expected a volley of abuse to be hurled at him too: hypocrite, bastard, anything at all that she could use to get even. Instead, she remained perfectly calm, perfectly distant. A far better punishment he thought.

He moved to retrieve her hand, but she only pulled it further away. After a short period of uncomfortable silence, Maria slowly climbed to her feet; her slender arms crossed across her flat stomach as if someone had just punched her, and began to walk away. She didn't even turn to look back at Jack; such was her sense of betrayal.

"Maria, wait."

She stopped.

"I like Samuel very much Jack and I only Raul's woman in Raul's mind," she replied, heading back to her room.

"Well you got your answer Jack," he whispered, watching her go.

~ ~ ~

Since Raul's visit, Raffa had been standing guard over the town square. For almost two hours now he'd been watching Sevilla from the courtyard wall, and he'd long since grown bored. Having polished off a few beers in order to relieve this boredom, he now stood beside the courtyard's gate, emptying his full bladder into one of the many bushes which were nearby.

The air was chilly that evening. A thick cloud of steam rose from the ground as he continued to relieve himself. He was thinking of all the things he could do once he had his share of the ransom money, when there came a loud bang against the courtyard gate.

Quickly zipping up his fly, he pressed an ear against the gate's thick wood. Again, the fist outside made firm contact. Could it be Raul? Were the rebels already in town, preparing to steal what had already been stolen?

"It's Samuel, let me in!"

"Are you sure?"

"Of course I'm bloody sure, now open the gate!" the voice continued. Raffa hesitated. It could be a trick. He could open the gate and find Raul facing him; shotgun in hand, its barrel pointing at his gullible head.

"You have the money?"

"Yes, I have the suitcase, now open the bloody gate!" Samuel almost screamed. Raffa thought about running for backup, but if it was Samuel outside, suitcase full of cash, then he wanted to get to the money before any of the other men.

"Okay, one second," he replied, lifting the gate's long, wooden barrier and then stepping back as the gate itself gently swung open. The empty square appeared. He could see the rows of distant buildings along its furthest perimeters, but no Samuel.

"Samuel?"

No answer. He took a step forward. The heavy gate continued to swing back. Across the square, houselights flickered. He was thinking how pretty they all looked when the sound of a pistol being cocked snapped him back into reality. From the shadows, off to his left, Samuel emerged, the gun in one hand, the suitcase held firmly in the other.

"Get back inside, c'mon, we haven't got all night."

Raffa did as Samuel asked. Both men stepped silently back into the courtyard. Lowering the suitcase to the ground, Samuel closed the gate himself. With the gun still pointing at Raffa's head, he made the Colombian replace the barrier.

"Now where's Jack?" Samuel asked, his eyes nervously darting back and forth across the courtyard, indeed almost everywhere except to look Raffa in the eye.

"He inside with the others, waiting for you."

"You sure? I'll blow your head off if you're telling me lies."

"I'm sure!" Raffa protested. Samuel kept the gun steady on the Colombian's head. He still couldn't believe he'd come back. He'd been halfway across town, his mind set on Bogota and then on toward Rio, when he'd suffered the massive guilt trip. He was angry, beyond angry. With all that money in the case he could have set himself up in Brazil for life, perhaps even returned to London to start up his own picture library.

And yet still, like some kind of naughty pup, he'd come crawling back. Despite all his resentment, he couldn't leave Jack and the others to face the music alone. He wasn't his father's son after all. He had a conscience, and the revelation irritated him.

"You okay?" Raffa mumbled. Although Samuel stood facing him, he appeared distant, his eyes vacant.

"Just take me to Jack," Samuel then ordered, waving for Raffa to move. He did, slowly at first, wary of the gun that was still fixed on his head.

On his return to the town square, Samuel had found Raul and a few others loitering near its centre, not far from the tree. For almost an hour he'd stuck to the shadows, the suitcase handle digging into his hand, and it was only by some miracle that he'd been able to navigate them and reach the gate without being seen. How they were going to escape town was an entirely different matter.

~ ~ ~

The strip club doors had been closed, the disgruntled punters told to leave. Now Leopold and his cohorts hung about the square like lost children awaiting fresh instruction. Raul wandered in amongst them, lost in thought himself. Other men would be in town soon. Not like Leopold, not like the handful of locals who he'd cajoled into joining them. They would be hard men, seasoned fighters. Men who'd known battle from their earliest years. One phone call was all it had taken, a few choice words into their commander's ear, the promise of ransom money to come once the Englishman was dead, the only real bait.

But Raul was also worried. Sevilla had always been his town, his to protect and occasionally plunder. Its citizens all knew him, feared him. He even had a few friends. He'd had big plans for

Sevilla. Now all that was at risk, and for what? Pride? Jealousy? What would stop the rebels from taking over his entire operation when eventually they did arrive? He'd been foolish then, rash in his desire for instant revenge. When the soldiers came he'd have to show them who was boss, push himself that little bit extra and so win their respect.

"How much longer we gotta wait?" Leopold nagged, having smoked the last of his cigarettes over forty minutes ago and now feeling irritable because of it.

"Be quiet," Raul snapped. He wasn't sure how long. Another hour. Maybe two. One thing was for certain, Jack and his friends would not be allowed to leave their convent until the soldiers did show, and only then, together, would they act swiftly to flush them out.

~ ~ ~

"You're a bloody fool Samuel!" Jack yelled, pacing up and down the room. He almost went to swing for him but managed to hold his temper in check. "A bloody fool!"

Inwardly, he'd been overjoyed at having his son back safe and well, but was still fuming over the boy's complete lack of discretion concerning Maria.

"I think you're going a little bit over the top here, Dad."

"Over the top! My main rival, local head of the FARC, caught you with his girl, and I'm going over the top?"

"I was just looking out for her that's all...She helped me out of a tight spot so..."

"So you thought you'd bed her!" Jack interrupted.

Maria, who'd been sitting quietly in the far corner listening to the argument, suddenly jumped up from her stool.

"I never sleep with him, you lie! Tell him Samuel."

Samuel, leaning against the room's door frame, was more than a little hurt by the ferocity of her denial.

"She's telling the truth Dad, we never..."

"Oh be quiet! That's not the bloody issue. In Raul's mind you and Maria have been together and that's that!"

"Well, let Raul think what he like, I don't care!" Maria continued, re-taking her stool. She'd still not forgiven Jack for his earlier accusations, and now she would definitely be ignoring him.

"Oh yes, you don't care young lady, but I'm the one who's going to have to get us out of this fix."

Their tiny room had become so jammed full of people it was difficult to walk even a few yards without bumping into somebody. Jack continued to pace up and down like he was on the verge of some great, never to be seen before discovery, at the same time trying to avoid Raffa and the other men who now sat about the floor, counting out their cash into large piles.

Jack was annoyed for one other very good reason. He'd banked on Samuel returning a lot earlier and now that Raul and a few of his cronies had pitched camp right outside, all the plans he'd made for their escape had become that extra bit difficult.

"It's all here!" Raffa suddenly announced, his pockets already stuffed to capacity with his share, the other men still busy filling theirs.

"Of course it's all there," Samuel replied, hoping nobody would miss the couple of grand that he'd slipped into his own back pocket.

Jack was now standing by the window. A large crowd had gathered outside, mostly young men, eager to get their hands on their slice of the cash. In their frustration, one or two had even begun to slap their palms against the dusted glass. All of them carried a weapon of some kind: Rifle, pistol, machete.

"You'd best go and pay these lot Raffa before they break in and take it all for themselves," Jack spoke, his head cocking toward the baying mob.

Raffa had already closed the suitcase and was making for the door, his own men close behind.

"You come also Jack?"

Jack shrugged.

"I may as well...Make sure everything is handled fairly."

Raffa smiled. The door was opened and together they stepped outside.

Curious, Maria hovered beside the window. As expected, Jack and Raffa had been quickly surrounded by the mob. Together, the crowd had then begun to drift toward the courtyard centre. She couldn't see the case or the money being exchanged, but only Raffa's quick hands darting this way and that in amongst the pressing bodies. Jack towered above them all, both his arms raised, appealing for some sort of calm.

"I think your father will take care of us Samuel."

"He only takes care of himself, I wouldn't go raising your hopes," he answered, now claiming Maria's stool for himself.

"You are too harsh on him...He talks about you a lot, all the time!"

Maria was looking hard at Samuel, ready to dissect his next answer, if and when it came. Samuel sensed it and backed off. Maria had other ideas.

"You were going to leave town weren't you? Take the cash all for yourself?"

"What if I was?"

"So, you were going to run out on your father!"

"I came back didn't I?"

"Maybe you get scared...Little boys can get scared."

"I had my reasons for coming back Maria, one very good reason."

"Don't say what I think you're going to say Samuel...Those kind of words can be dangerous."

"Maria..."

Jack burst back into the room, stuffing his mobile into his jacket pocket.

"Right, you both get yourselves a good night's kip."

"Why? What's going on?" Samuel questioned, annoyed with the interruption.

"Because we leave first thing tomorrow son," Jack replied, standing next to Maria.

"I sure hope you know what you're doing."

"Certainly I know what I'm doing, please Samuel, show a little more faith in your old man...Now, I shall be taking the room next door...Maria? Will you be staying put?"

Samuel knew what her reply was going to be and braced himself for the rejection.

"I would like my own room tonight Jack," she replied, sending Samuel's mood plummeting even further. Jack threw him a wistful glance.

"Not a problem Maria, we have a spare room a couple of doors down."

"Yeah, well, sweet dreams Maria," Samuel quipped as they made for the door. She ignored him.

"You'll be okay won't you son?"

Samuel nodded.

"Then sleep well...We'll see you in the morning, and don't worry, I have everything under control," Jack finished, pulling open the door and stepping outside with Maria.

"Sure, you have everything under control."

Pretending not to hear, Jack closed the door.

Samuel had not found much difficulty in falling asleep that evening. The day's stressful events had worked far better than any sleeping tablet could ever hope to do, and he'd slipped quietly away only moments after Jack and Maria had left. He dreamed. He dreamed of his father strolling across the convent's wide courtyard toward its gateway. It stood open. To his surprise, Raul stood beneath its tall arch, and both men had begun to speak. Samuel could even hear the conversation. Jack was telling Raul what a fine son he'd bought into the world and that he would do anything to make sure no harm came to him. The large Colombian seemed to listen intently, several times nodding his head as the conversation progressed, and as he listened, Samuel began to wander if Raul himself had a father, a good father like his own.

"Samuel..."

He woke in time to feel the second, delicate kiss plant itself against the tip of his nose. Maria sat watching over him, her long, dark curls freely draped over her white nightgown. She looked concerned, as if he was going to tell her to leave at any given moment.

"I came to say I am sorry."

Pulling back the bed's covers, he shifted over to make room.

"Are you cold?"

"A little."

He gave the free space next to him a gentle pat. Pulling her nightdress down so that it rode just beneath her knees, she snuggled up beside him. For a time they laid in silence, her smaller frame wrapped up in his, her face pressed against his chest, listening to the rhythm of his heartbeat.

"Will you talk to him?"

"I don't think we have a lot to talk about."

"He had his reasons Samuel, good reasons."

"Doesn't mean I have to listen to them. My father is a conman Maria. If he told you he'd been to the moon and back you'd believe it. He's very good at telling lies."

Undeterred, Maria began to litter his neck with soft kisses.

"Talk to him...For me."

"And if I do?"

Without warning, she bought her hand up between his legs, leaning over as she did to kiss his lips.

"Look at me."

She did. Slowly, he ran a hand down the warm, smooth skin of her belly, teasing her legs to part as his fingers dived between her slender thighs. He felt the wetness which lived between her thighs, pressing harder now with each reach.

"You like that?" he whispered, enjoying her moist warmth.

She didn't answer. She didn't have to. Her trembling fingers, already at work, hovered across her cherry red nipples. Her passion blossoming, she squeezed her firm breasts together and groaned each time Samuel's fingers entered her.

"Get inside me," she demanded, her hands abandoning her own flesh to claw at his lower back. Taking her head firmly in both hands, he ran his tongue gently across the arch of her neck, placing himself carefully between her open thighs.

"Look at me," he repeated, this time more forcefully. Again, she did, and groaned each time he burrowed deeper into her. His hands then moved to cup both her breasts, his tongue working small, delicate circles around the tips of her large nipples. She locked her strong legs tight about his waist as if trying to squeeze the very life out of him. Their mutual assault continued, and when it was all over, their fires at last satisfied, if not entirely extinguished, they remained entangled, at peace, until the following day.

13

Face To Face

"Jesus Christ! Never grow old Raffa, never grow old," Jack cursed as he sat upright. He'd fallen asleep beside what remained of the bonfire and now he'd begun to regret the decision.

"Too late for me Jack, I already fifty," Raffa replied, taking hold of Jack's arm and helping him to stand. It was early morning, the sky above the courtyard walls still a light grey in colour. Sleeping men littered the entire sanctuary. Each man had been paid his fair share of the ransom money, and a great deal of celebrating had been done the night previous.

Jack and Raffa wandered amongst the sleepers, Jack dusting down his shirt, Raffa occasionally stopping to jab one of the men with his boot. If any of them stirred it was no more than a reflex action. Too much beer had been drunk. They would sleep until late afternoon.

"Stupid buggers, the rebels will take all their cash when they get here," Jack predicted. He was right and Raffa nodded thoughtfully as they strolled along. The men had no real discipline, unlike the rebels. It was one good reason why they'd stay poor farmers for the rest of their days, long after Jack had gone.

"You need to go soon Jack," Raffa spoke, stopping walking, having seen enough of the rabble at his feet.

"You do have a way out?" he continued, as they both headed back toward their rooms.

Samuel and Maria, dog tired, were stepping from their own room as both the men approached. Jack glanced at his watch.

"If all goes to plan...Ten, twenty minutes maybe."

"The rebel soldiers are with Raul now Jack. A dozen or so, not as many as we'd feared."

Jack sighed.

"I'm afraid one rebel is worth two of ours, and all of them will be too busy recovering from their hangovers to be much use to us."

"Then I hope your plan is a good one."

"Well, whatever happens Raffa, it should be fun!"

"And the hostages?"

"Coming with me. I couldn't leave the poor devils here, no telling what might happen to them."

Samuel and Maria were still rubbing the sleep from their eyes as both parties reached one another.

"Morning," Samuel was the first to mumble.

"And a good morning to you too...Sleep well?" Jack teased, eyeing Maria who clung to Samuel's waist. She looked a long way from being awake herself.

"Not bad, under the circumstances...When do we leave?"

"Soon, so you'd best get yourselves some breakfast, could be your last meal for quite some time."

"I'll go and check on Raul," Raffa added, jogging over toward the courtyard wall.

"Going to let us in on your wonderful plan of escape?" Samuel questioned, still not entirely happy at having to put all his faith in his father.

"Just leave that one to me Sammy and don't worry."

"Well I think we have a right to know Jack...Christ, our lives are on the line here too you know!"

Jack held up his hand.

"I'm not going to argue this one, now go and make Maria some breakfast while I go and check on our American friends," he finished, turning quickly. As he turned, Maria gave Samuel a painful jab to his ribs with her elbow.

"Dad..."

"Yes son?"

"Would it be okay to talk? I mean a little later on."

Jack smiled.

"Of course it would, but let's just concentrate on leaving Sevilla first, that okay with you?"

"Sure, no problem," Samuel answered. As he replied his father turned again and headed toward the cell trapdoor.

"Gracias," Maria spoke, giving Samuel a peck on his cheek.

~ ~ ~

"Come on, time to get up!" Jack barked, throwing off the boy's dirty sheets. Time was running out and Jack was in no mood for waiting.

"Hell, what's going on?"

Jack was kneeling beside Joseph, trying to unlock his ankle chains. The lock had become rusted over time and now the key struggled to fit inside.

"Blasted thing!"

"Is it mealtime already?" Joe mumbled, barely awake.

"No, not meal time young Joe. It's home time."

At the mention of the word home, the cell's other two remaining hostages began to stir. Joseph simply stared at Jack. Over the passing weeks he'd managed to convince himself that he'd been disowned by his parents, and now Jack's news genuinely surprised him.

"You mean dad paid up? He actually paid up?"

"Luckily for you, yes."

"I'm going home! I'm going home!"

At last the key slipped into the lock. A second later and the boy's chains had fallen loose.

"Now be careful Joseph, you'll probably feel a little unsteady at first," Jack warned, taking Joseph's hand and helping him to stand. The boy didn't listen and almost fell twice. Eventually, with Jack supporting him, he managed to find his feet and lean against the cell wall.

"I can't believe I'm ge'tin' outa here, I knew pops wouldn't let me down...I just knew it!" he continued to babble, bending over to give his sore ankles a good rub.

"Hey! What about the rest of us?" a thick New York accent complained. Having thrown off his own sheets Michael now crawled into the middle of the cell. A single shaft of sunlight fell into the cell through the barred window directly above and, reaching its edge, he stopped, his eyes too sensitive to risk going any further.

As with Joseph, Jack knelt beside him, once again fishing about in his pockets, looking for the right key.

"When do I get to go home? Can you tell me that one Jack?"

"You all get to go free."

A pause.

"All of us? Dave too?"

"That's what I just said," Jack replied, pulling out the correct key and placing it carefully into

Michael's ankle lock. The lock was in far better condition than Joseph's and so entered first time.

"I thought you couldn't find our folks? You said you couldn't find anybody!"

"Quite true."

"Then I don't get it Jack, why the sudden change of heart? There's gotta be a catch here somewhere."

"No catch young man, no catch."

But Michael wasn't convinced. As hard as Jack and Shelley had tried, neither of them had been able to locate his parents, or anybody else for that matter. Bundles of letters had been sent, telephone numbers dialled, but with no success. The same had applied to David. It was mostly Jack's fault. Both young men were a good deal older than Joseph, almost ten years, and neither of them had bothered to stay in touch with their families or friends.

Jack had bumped into them in one of Sevilla's bars. Not surprisingly, they'd all got very drunk that evening, and although they'd each boasted of individual wealth, once Jack had been able to coax them back to the convent, plied their systems with even more booze, it hadn't taken a sober Shelley long to see clean through their bullshit and uncover the awful truth. They were both broke; both of them bumming through South America on what little cash they had left. By then it was too late. Jack had never liked to admit defeat, let alone be proven wrong, and come the following afternoon, once his terrible hangover had cleared up, he'd insisted on keeping the pair until at least somebody they knew found the decency to pay a ransom. So far almost a month had slipped by without a word of reply from anybody.

"C'mon Davey boy, your turn next," Jack continued, walking toward the far end of the cell. Dave had spent most of his days asleep, but now even he was wide awake.

"You're not shittin' us right? We really ge'tin' out this flea pit?"

"For the last time of asking, yes!"

"But who paid our ransom?"

"Long story."

"Well, you seem edgy to me pal, something's up!" Michael continued, now hovering behind Jack's right shoulder. He was the most outspoken of the three Americans and the one most likely to cause trouble. Although smaller in build than Jack, he was fairly stocky and boasted two enormous fists.

"Nothing is up Michael!"

"Maybe nobody's paid our ransom. You guys thought of that one?" Joseph suddenly babbled, still marooned against the cell wall,

"Maybe they gonna execute us!"

"Don't be so bloody stupid!" Jack snapped, having unlocked Dave's chains.

"Then just answer the damn question, who's paid up?"

Both the New Yorker boys were third generation Irish; full of lip, but with the tempers to back it up. Quickly, not wanting the situation to escalate, Jack pulled his pistol from out his belt and did a mini sweep with it from Dave's face through to Joseph's. As the gun passed, each man froze.

"We do have a spot of bother on our hands gentlemen, but nothing for you to worry about..."

"That's easy for you to say, you even gonna tell us what sorta trouble we in?" Michael interrupted, his face turning red, almost as red as his wavy hair. Carefully, Jack cocked the pistol.

"As long as you all listen to me, do exactly what I say, when I say, we can all be out of town within a few hours."

"I guess we just gotta take your word on that one Jack!" Michael spoke. At that moment he didn't much care for the gun and was half tempted to storm Jack there and then. The older man was quick to see this in his eyes and trained the weapon directly onto his pale forehead.

"I've given you my answer son."

If it was a battle of wills the boy was after then Jack would make sure he came out on top.

"Now, if you'd all like to climb the ladder, we can be on our merry way. This damp cellar plays havoc with my chest."

"Yeah, well join the club pal," Joseph chipped in, still giving one of his ankles a gentle rub.

With a little shake of the pistol, all three men were made to head for the ladder. Jack kept himself a safe distance behind the small group, the pistol held steady as he watched them climb toward the courtyard.

"Don't we even get a weapon to defend ourselves? A knife? A stick? Anything?" Michael questioned, already halfway up.

"Just stop your whining and get moving," came Jack's sharp reply as he stepped onto the ladder himself.

~ ~ ~

The small rebel faction had arrived in town not long before dawn. Raffa, still on guard at that time, had watched them gather. He'd counted ten soldiers in all. They were fit, young looking specimens, and by the time Jack and his three hostages had left the underground cell, these soldiers, led by Raul, had begun a slow advance across the square.

"You know something boys, at times like this I feel like Othello!" Jack boomed, having reached Raffa.

"What he say?" Raffa inquired. He didn't like it when Jack started to talk funny. It made him feel uneasy.

"I think it's Shakespeare," Samuel replied. "At least his own version."

"I'm stood before the Venetian crowds and all I can see are monkeys and goats!" Jack finished, watching the rebels slow advance; leaning himself against one of the wall's thick turrets.

Having left the Americans with some of his more trusted Colombians, Jack, together with Samuel had decided to join Raffa as he kept watch over the square. Now as Raul approached, Raffa made his way back down into the courtyard and tried to wake the rest of Jack's men from their drunken slumber. It was no use and eventually he gave up trying.

"You've found a decent girl in Maria you know, you should try and keep hold of her...Take it from me, girls like her don't come around so often."

"Like the way you stood by my mother?"

Jack shook his head and very nearly chuckled.

"Don't you ever stop? Can't you at least try and forget what happened? All this resentment can't be healthy for you."

"I think the word you were looking for was forgive, and no, I couldn't just forget, that would be letting you off the hook."

Samuel kept his eyes on the square. The soldiers were already nearing its centre and it wouldn't be long before they were standing right outside the convent gates.

"Did you even love her?"

"For a time, but not enough, not in the way she deserved. Your mother deserved better."

"I've often wondered what it would be like to leave behind a family that you loved. It couldn't have been easy."

"I'm not sure we have the time for this Samuel."

"Before you left, those early years, you must have been content?"

Not wanting the argument, Jack turned away. Raul and his tribe were very close now. They weren't what he'd expected either. Although in the main they were hard looking men, Jack could see at least two female fighters within the group, and one of the boys looked no older than fourteen. All of them walked confidently toward the convent, however, their guns slung proudly over their shoulders. Raul and Leopold led the way, Raul almost casual in his approach.

"You can't keep running Dad, sooner or later you'll have to stop and face the past. Talk to me."

Jack sighed, his eyes still fixed on the square, his fingers picking at the stone wall.

"The thing is Samuel, I wasn't content. Not really. Some men can settle, but not me. I wanted something more out of life. I wanted to ring it dry and soak myself in all her pleasures! I'm a selfish bastard Samuel. I've always been that way. You were better off without me!"

He turned around to face his son, a cold look of despair having crept into his eyes. There was no hiding it.

"Please try and understand Samuel, if I had stayed, the chances are you'd be standing here right now berating me for having led you into a life of crime and hating me for it!"

"You don't know that for certain."

Jack slammed his fist against the wall.

"Damn it! I do! Others steal out of necessity. I do it for fun, for the rush, for the sheer hell of it! Believe me, in leaving, I did you all a favour. If it's an apology that you're after son, then I'm sorry, I truly am."

Raffa, who'd been listening to their argument for some time, standing some distance away, now decided to join them.

"Jack..."

"It's okay Raffa, I see them," Jack replied. Raul and his miniature army were now waiting patiently below.

"Have I come at a bad time Senor Locke?" Raul suddenly bellowed.

"Don't be silly Raul. It's always a pleasure to see your ugly mug," Jack replied.

"Very funny, but will you still be laughing when you hand me over your son?"

"My boy and the girl stay here."

Raul nodded.

"I had a feeling you were going to say that, just as well I brought some friends along."

"Do they fight as well as you talk?"

"Even better, you will find that out soon enough."

"Let me finish him now..." Samuel blasted, reaching for his pistol. Jack moved quicker and grabbed his hand.

"Control yourself, you wouldn't stand a chance."

"Everything alright Senor Locke? Your son looks a little nervous."

Jack pushed his son away from the wall.

"Before we all go losing our heads Raul, I thought maybe we could talk. I have a second offer that you may find of some interest."

Barely listening, Raul cleared his throat and spat what had been collected into the dust.

"So very tedious," he whispered toward the soldiers.

"I tell you already what I want...I not interested in anything else that you may or may not have!"

"Well, I think I could change your mind...Let's say I come down there and chat face to face."

"Face to face?" Raul replied, genuinely surprised by the offer.

"That's what I said."

"Are you nuts?" Samuel exploded, blocking Jack's path even before he had a chance to move.

"They'll shoot you on sight!"

Jack simply glanced at his watch. Time was pressing. No time left to argue. Raul, conscious of looking like a coward in front of his troops, nodded.

"Very well, face to face it is, but be warned, any trouble and you all die!"

"Understood perfectly Raul. I just want to talk. I give you my word they'll be no funny business."

"I'm not letting you do this," Samuel interrupted, this time stepping closer toward his father and placing the palm of his hand against his chest.

"You're just asking for a bullet!"

Without replying, Jack brushed him easily to one side and again checked his watch.

"Dad, please!"

"Oh, will you please stop fretting child! I'm not looking to get shot! Far from it. I have a plan you see. It's a very secret plan that will save all our bacon. Now, will you please be a good fellow Samuel and just follow my lead? "

"But you just..."

"The key to any magic trick young man is in its preparation."

Samuel stared at him blankly.

"Magic trick? What are you twittering on about?"

"I don't intend to go down there alone; you're coming with me too. Indeed I think it's high time we all made a move, so be a good lad and go fetch Maria will you?"

"Maria? Now listen, we're not taking..."

"Oh yes we are Samuel," Jack broke in, already disappearing down the ladder.

"Now go fetch her!"

"I think your father has gone loco!" Raffa added, having caught them both up.

Samuel watched Jack stride across the courtyard, dishing out his orders to anybody who'd listen, and didn't argue the point. His father was mad, perfectly mad.

~ ~ ~

Save for the fact that Jack and his men had also gone without food and water for many days during their stay in Sevilla, Maria would have found it easy to hate the Englishman. As they huddled together in her tiny room, each of the Americans looked weak and pale. Damping her thick cloth into the small bowl of warm water for a second time, she gently patted Joseph's raw ankles.

"Locke is gonna pay for this," one of his friends spoke. He'd introduced himself over an hour ago but she'd already forgotten his name.

"If we ever get outa this alive, if I ever bump into him. I swear, that guy will die!" Michael continued, taking a long sip from the only bottle of water Maria's room had boasted.

The third American, the eldest amongst the three, slowly nodded his head. Maria remembered his name because he'd been the only one to say thank you when she'd offered him a drink from the bottle of water. He'd also looked the most ill when Jack's men had shuffled him inside, and so the one who'd caused her the most concern. David's light, blue eyes were on her now. He'd been looking at her for some time, his expression perplexed.

"I think I seen you before some place."

Maria timidly shook her head. He was right but she didn't want to admit the fact. She thought she'd seen him before too, and only when he'd been forced to sit in front of her had she been able to place the face. David and his friend had both visited Raul's strip club several months ago, probably on the same night Jack had taken them hostage. Joseph and Michael were now staring at her too, David even beginning to wiggle a dirty finger in her direction.

"Yeah, I'm sure I seen your face before. Just give me a second and I'll have it."

Maria lowered her eyes, ringing out the cloth into the bowl. Joseph's ankles were at least clean but she was still worried about infection. The cuts which were sprinkled above his feet weren't deep but the heavy chains had caused so many wounds he would have to see a doctor just as soon as they reached a safe haven.

"Have you lived in Sevilla all your life?" Joseph asked, already having developed a small crush on Maria.

"All my life."

"You never thought of going to some other town? Jeez, I think I'd go nuts staying in a place like this for too long."

"If I had your money I would."

At that moment, Samuel stepped into the room, his pistol tucked tightly inside his trouser belt. Maria was certain it was done for effect. She couldn't blame Samuel either. Since the

Americans had arrived, a great deal of their grievances had centred on Jack and his son.

"Well, look who it is!" Michael was the first to speak, his eyes suddenly intense as Samuel had appeared.

"The traitor in our midst."

"We're leaving soon Maria. You think these guys will be ready?"

"Oh, sure, we'll be ready pal, can't wait to get our feet moving again. Being holed up in a stinking cell kinda has that effect you know," Michael broke in. Feeling a little stronger he would have laid Samuel out a long time ago. As it was he remained sitting against the wall.

"What about the boy?"

Samuel was looking directly at Joseph as he spoke.

"The boy will be just fine!" Joe snapped back.

"His ankles are in a bad way but I think he'll make it."

"I'll make it alright, all the way to Jack!"

"Where is your father Samuel?" Maria continued, carefully rolling Joseph's trouser legs back down.

"Yeah, where's Jack, Sammy? I think we'd all like to know that one," Michael went on. Samuel didn't know. After Jack had left the courtyard wall he'd quickly lost sight of him.

"Just be ready for when I get back Maria," he replied, his fragile temper already beginning to crack under the American's hostility.

Samuel found his father in the chapel. Jack hadn't taken to drinking from the bottles of wine, but was instead kneeling before its empty altar, hands gripped tightly together, mumbling a few words. The sight frightened Samuel more than anything else he'd seen that day and so he decided not to gate crash the meditation.

As Samuel left the chapel, Raffa and Saul were busy waking the remaining Colombians. They wandered about the courtyard, their shaky hands either tending to their sore heads or their aching ribs. Maria appeared from her room as Samuel was making his way toward Raffa. His back was turned from her and she'd tugged the collar of his shirt.

"How will these men fight? Not one can hold a gun steady!" she protested.

Samuel could only shrug.

"I guess Jack has it all under control. He mumbled something about a plan."

They were empty words and did nothing to comfort Maria who was feeling so nervous she'd very nearly made herself sick.

Soon after Maria's observation, Jack bounced out the chapel, his haggard face all smiles. Samuel wished he could drop the mask.

"Sorry to keep you both waiting."

"Seeking absolution?" Samuel poked.

"Don't be silly, just taking a final tipple. I stumbled across a lovely vintage that I hadn't tried before."

"Taste good?"

"Wonderful stuff!"

"Shame your men can't handle their drink as well."

"Not my men. Not any more. They have their money. They knew the risks Samuel. On their own now I'm afraid."

"And what about Raffa?"

"Sod Raffa."

Raffa spotted Jack and jogged quickly toward him.

"Raul will be getting impatient. We must leave soon Jack."

Jack was ready to reply when a little bleep from his mobile went off. He took the phone from his pocket and began to read the short text which had been sent. He smiled.

"Yes, now would be a very good time to leave."

~ ~ ~

Free at last from their superior's gaze, the two female soldiers were now allowed to flaunt their curves without any fear of reprisal. Having thrown off their heavy combat jackets they strolled about the square in nothing more than T-shirts and tight shorts. The rebel army didn't allow male and female soldiers to mix; a rule that was strictly obeyed. Anybody caught breaking it faced severe punishment. During his time with the rebels, Raul had been ordered to execute several soldiers who'd crossed this line, younger members whose only crime was to have found some solace in each other.

As the girls swung their hips the male fighters began to whistle. Leopold eyed the women closely as they put themselves on show. Now that he was in charge, Raul let them. He could see nothing wrong. He was busy clearing out the barrel of his pistol when the convent gates began to open. Jack's earlier offer had come as a complete surprise and Raul could not help thinking that this sly old fox would have some trick up his sleeve.

He'd agreed to meet because he'd been curious, but was more than ready to put the Englishman in his place as and when the situation required. The gates came to a gentle rest. The rebel soldiers, having abandoned their flirting, stood prepared with their weapons.

"What do we do now Raul?" Leopold asked, sticking close by his boss. Leopold had never fought a battle in his life, certainly no gun battle, and the thought of having to actually fight, turned his puny stomach inside out. His hands shook. He clung to his pistol like a man holding onto a rattlesnake and would not stop shaking. The soldiers quickly surrounded him, their automatic rifles at the ready. Far from making Leopold feel more secure however, their presence only turned his bubbling fear into a full blown panic. He tugged violently at Raul's shirt sleeve.

"Raul? Do I start shooting now?"

A posse of men with Jack at their helm were stepping from the courtyard. Raul's keen, hawkish eyes began a search for Maria amongst the throng, but were unable to find her.

"Raul. God damn it. Do I shoot them now?"

Leopold was shaking so bad he was almost ready to faint, and from the irritated looks on the faces of the gathered rebels, they seemed almost ready to shoot him and have done with it. Somehow Raul managed to keep his cool. After all this was over, after he'd killed off the competition, he swore he'd slit open Leopold's scrawny, nagging throat himself. But that time would come. For now, he would need to concentrate.

"First we talk to them Leopold. First we talk," he eventually replied, stepping forward.

"Talk, good...That sounds good, real good."

14

Showdown

Jack's eyes carefully studied the approaching soldiers. His own motley band stuck close by, and as the two groups neared not a single word could be heard. It was the usual mixture of fear and high excitement which did it, and only when the bullets began to fly would the rhetoric kick in.

Of course Jack's only real concern was for Samuel, and as long as he could keep Raul talking, keep stalling for valuable time, without making their enemies too suspicious, well then maybe, just maybe, his secret plan could work.

His eyes fixed on Raul. Everything he knew about the man he'd been told directly by the farmers in his employ or through the brief conversations he'd had with Sevilla's locals. Jack could only hope that his nemeses was a good listener who didn't like to ask too many awkward questions as this would be important if they were all going to make it out of Sevilla alive that evening. A handful of cautious strides later and both men stood inches from one another. Jack was the first to speak:

"I heard you were good looking Raul...People can be such liars!"

Raul grinned. Even the rebels, not noted for their humour in tight situations like these, chuckled at the remark. Leopold thought about smiling but didn't want to tempt fate. Instead, he gripped his tiny pistol even tighter and continued to pray that he would never have to use it – not ever.

"I didn't come here to tell jokes Senor Locke."

"But who was telling jokes?"

Another ripple of laughter ran through the rebel ranks. This time however Raul's expression remained serious. He had a funny, twisted kind of respect for Jack and he was anxious not to end up liking the man. It was always more difficult to kill a man that you'd actually come to like. He began to think of all the ransom money Jack would have collected, and soon found it much easier to hate him.

"Shall we talk seriously Jack?"

"Isn't that why we're here? To chat?" Jack replied, glancing at Raul's men, their impressive array of guns in particular. He'd been right from word go. His own men wouldn't stand a chance against this lot. The rebels knew it and stood proudly to attention as they faced Jack and his scruffy looking entourage.

At the very back of this group, just inside the convent walls, Samuel and Maria stood holding one another. They'd been told to stay well out of sight, and although neither of them had the faintest inkling what wonderful trick was up Jack's sleeve, they'd both done as Jack had asked, strangely confident in his ability to get them out of trouble. 'Just do what I say when I say,' had been their only instruction, and so far both had been happy to play along.

Occasionally, as Raul raised his voice, Maria buried her head into Samuel's chest. She felt confused and terribly afraid. She hated Raul; had come to hate all the things he'd done to her over the years, and loathed the fact that from now on, wherever she went, with whoever she ended up with, Raul would still be a part of her personnel history, a large bundle of unhappy memories that would have to be pushed to the very back of her mind any time the words past relationships were mentioned, or whenever she was feeling particularly low and had begun to dwell on her years in Sevilla. It almost made her want to stay in town. What was the point in leaving? Raul would be with her, wherever she went.

"I'm sure we can reach a compromise Raul," Jack continued, trying his best to engage the Colombian in conversation. For the time being, the larger man seemed content to listen. And why not? Of the two, he'd soon be calling all the shots.

"First you hand me Romeo and Juliet...Then maybe we talk."

"Well that wasn't quite what I had in mind Raul...You see I don't think I could ever betray my son in that way, or the girl for that matter. I haven't known her long, but she's sort of grown on me."

"Then what have you to offer?"

"I'll give you the Americans, plus whatever ransoms they can attract."

Raul smiled, as did one or two of the rebels. It all sounded so very simple.

"And If I refuse?"

Jack paused, trying to weigh up how far he could push his adversary.

"Then I suppose we all come to blows!"

At that point Raul's troops burst into laughter.

"You can see for yourself Jack that we are far stronger."

"Maybe so, but we'll take a shed load of your people with us if you do refuse to play ball."

The laughter began to peter out. Raul's broad grin also faded.

"We could have made a great deal of money for ourselves if only your son had learnt to behave himself. It is a shame it has to end like this."

"For what it's worth Raul, Samuel swears blind he never touched your girl. I believe him," Jack lied.

"I know what I saw."

"What you think you saw."

Raul shook his head. No amount of talk would change his mind. Samuel was going to pay and it was all just a matter of time.

"I give you one last chance Jack...Stop screwing with my head."

For a split second, Jack's eyes shot off beyond Raul. He was running short on talk and only when he spotted the bus approaching them at great speed from across the square did he begin to relax.

"I've said all I've come to say Raul, the next move is entirely up to you," he replied, taking a cautious step back toward the relative safety of his own men; wishing the bus would hurry up.

Raul and the rebels were beginning to look very serious when the sound of the bus engine caught their collective ear. Suddenly curious, Raul turned slowly to find the cause of the noise.

"Jack?"

As the bus raced toward them, the rebels quickly raised their weapons. Caught in two minds, some pointed them at the oncoming bus, while others levelled theirs at Jack. All of them looked bemused. At the right moment, Jack raised his arms and appealed for calm.

"Tell them to lower their weapons Raul, the bus is empty."

"What game is this?"

"No game Raul, no game."

Something in Jack's soothing tone reassured the Colombian, and as the bus came to a halt some feet from both parties, Raul motioned his men to lower their weapons. Reluctantly, they did. The Englishman had been telling the truth. Apart from its nervous looking driver, the bus did appear to be empty.

"This is my final offer Raul."

"A bus! You offer me this?" Raul yelled, spinning back around to face Jack. Once again a ripple of laughter ran through the group. Calmly, Jack strolled through them.

"Not just the bus Raul, something far better than that," he replied, sticking his hand into his pocket and fishing out a large pair of keys. He now stood directly beside the bus, facing Raul and the others.

"This old beauty is far from empty!"

Kneeling down so that he was level with the baggage compartment, Jack slipped the key into its lock. Once more, the rebels raised their automatic rifles, as if expecting a flurry of men to burst out once the compartment door had been opened. Even Raul's pistol now trained itself toward the ageing Englishman. Carefully, so as not to cause even more concern, Jack lowered the door.

"Well, there you go Raul, my final offer, what say you now?"

Still more than a little suspicious, Raul and his soldiers shuffled forward, each of them speechless.

~ ~ ~

"What is going on?" Maria questioned, her arm looped through Samuel's arms as they both stood watching Jack's strange theatrical performance from beside the convent gates. Samuel wasn't sure. He couldn't see his father clearly, only the band of rebels who'd begun to crowd Jack and the bus.

"Samuel? Answer me!" Maria persisted. She couldn't stand the waiting any longer.

"I'm not sure Maria," came Samuel's honest reply. Everybody's attention was now focused on the bus, and it was something he couldn't explain.

"We go and drive away in that?" Maria continued. "It looks very old to me!"

"I think that could be the general idea," Samuel spoke, trying desperately to find his father in amongst the melee. For the time being, too many bodies blocked his view.

"Then why we wait so long?"

"Look, Maria..."

Before he could finish, the band of rebels unexpectedly parted. A second later and Jack appeared, both his arms held aloft, waving Samuel and Maria forward.

"You think it is safe?"

"Probably not," Samuel replied, grabbing hold of Maria's hand and pulling her toward the bus.

They both shook somewhat as they approached, but neither of them noticed much. Instead, they kept their eyes and hopes on Jack, and just prayed that he knew what he was doing.

"This stuff has gotta be worth thousands," Leopold proclaimed, peering into the buses large baggage compartment

"Perhaps more," Raul added, reaching deep into the murky hold to retrieve one of its many, unusual treasures.

In spite of the shadows, the compartment's heart shone with a faint silvery, sometimes golden glow. At first Raul wasn't sure what he'd retrieved until his hand was clear of the hold, and he was allowed to study his new prize in more detail.

"An Inca relic," Raul muttered.

"It's beautiful," Maria whispered, having pushed herself to the very edge of the crowd. Carefully, Raul cradled the tiny statue in the palm of his hand; gently peeling back those layers of soft fabric which had been wrapped about the figurine.

"The cloth is just as valuable," Jack added, leaning into the bus himself to collect one of the objects. Seeing this, it wasn't long before the rebel soldiers followed his lead and threw themselves headlong into the compartment.

"Where you find these Locke?" Raul wanted to know. The statue's cloth was so fine; its texture was barely noticeable to his touch. Jack, having rescued a golden figurine for himself, now pushed his way back through the jostling soldiers.

"Well, that would be telling old man. Needless to say it's amazing what the local Indians will show you if you pay them enough...Colombia's jungles are still rich in history!"

"Cortez would have been proud," Raul replied, running a finger along the head of the statue, where a blaze of red bird feather had been attached.

"I'm impressed Raul, I didn't think history would be your strong point."

"South America is my home Senor. You must remember that."

"Fair enough."

Unable to simply stand and watch a moment longer, Samuel had taken a statue for himself. Maria removed its fine cloth and was busy running the delicate material through her fingers.

"It's called qompi," Jack enlightened.

"Que?"

"The cloth dear, qompi, as important to the Incas as gold and literature had been to the Spaniards. Beautiful stuff isn't it?"

"Is it worth anything?" Michael interrupted, having managed to navigate a way through the rebels along with the other two hostages. Saul and Raffa shadowed them closely, Joseph in particular. Seeing the young man as the lesser of several evils, Jack had entrusted him with the suitcase.

"Typical bloody yank! May I remind you that there is more to life than just cash!"

"Hell! You're a fine one to talk," David interrupted.

Jack simply ignored him and continued his sermon.

"Can't you even try to appreciate what we have here? The craftsmanship, the history!"

Not bothering to reply, Michael began to rip away the statue's delicate cloth to get a better view of the silver beneath. Jack, seeing this as an act of mindless vandalism, was about ready to lecture him further, when he felt the barrel of Raul's shotgun pressing into the small of his back. He sighed.

"Oh, how very predictable."

"Turn around please Senor Locke."

Very slowly, Jack did. By this time, Maria and Samuel were standing next to the Colombian, Leopold trying his best to aim his pistol at them. His earlier shakes had returned with full vigour and it seemed more likely that he would miss the young lovers rather than hit the target successfully. Keeping his cool intact, Jack replied:

"Now Raul, I thought we'd come to some sort of understanding?"

"That's all very good Senor, but I would rather keep all the treasure for myself. A far better deal."

"I think you'll find you've miscalculated."

"Miscalculated?"

"Miguel!" Jack suddenly yelled, glancing toward the bus. Its front window shot open, and soon the driver was peering through, his own shotgun now trained on Raul's sweaty forehead.

"I would advise caution old boy; Miguel here is an excellent shot!"

"You crazy? My men will wipe you out!"

"Oh really?"

Raul's nervous eyes were already sneaking past Jack's large frame, watching with a gloomy sense of horror the terrible scene that was beginning to take shape behind him. Casually, Jack stepped to one side.

"How very predictable," he repeated, knowing exactly what was going to happen next.

Before them, one or two of the rebel soldiers, noting that their nearest colleague now carried slightly more loot than himself, had suddenly decided to take offence and confront. Quite soon, all of the soldiers were looking at each other's pile and feeling either very annoyed at what they saw, or quite happy with the amount they'd been able to pilfer. The most aggrieved amongst them dropped their loot and picked up the nearest rifle; quickly pointing it at whoever they felt had become too greedy.

Seeing this, Raffa's men could only follow their lead and soon an uneasy standoff had evolved between the two groups. Caught somewhere in the middle, the three Americans huddled together and prayed that everyone kept their heads. Jack smiled: His plan had worked perfectly so far.

"I think your men have other things on their minds Raul."

"What the hell are you doing? Damn it! You work for me!" the Colombian raged, wondering what to do next. His options looked limited. The rebels didn't want to listen. Jack smiled.

"Something Cortez told the Aztec's springs to mind...Now what was it?"

"My men suffer from a disease of the heart which can only be cured by gold," Raul dolefully replied, his eyes still on the soldiers, expecting their first gunshot to erupt at any moment.

"Well remembered Raul, you should have taught history, you're very good at it."

"Boss? Do I shoot them now?" Leopold still had Samuel and Maria in his sights and wasn't sure what to do next.

"Let them go."

"But boss!"

"Just do what I say Leopold!"

Picking his moment perfectly, Samuel swung a fist at the American's head. The punch connected with the ridge of Leopold's elongated nose, and he was sent crashing to the ground, thick blood splashing from both his nostrils and across his face before he'd even reached the dust.

"Sweet shot," Jack praised, slowly backing away from Raul, the shotgun still trained on him. Very slowly, the Colombian shook his head, not surprised by Leopold's fate.

"Idiot!" he mumbled.

"Now, on the bloody bus!" Jack ordered, using his free hand to help usher Maria aboard. Almost on the point of tears, Raul had begun to pick at the statue. He was about to fling it into the dust when something caught his attention. He froze, his mouth opening slightly. His fingernails were now covered in tiny golden flakes.

"Wait a second. Damn it! These are fakes!"

"On the bloody bus!" Jack yelled for a second time, waving Michael and David forward. The two Americans gladly dropped their loot and sprinted for the bus.

"Dad?"

Jack grinned.

"Well of course the statues are bloody fakes. Do you think I'd need the case if they were real?"

"You're mad. Completely mad!"

Having recovered from his earlier punch, Leopold was just in time to watch Jack slam the buses doors.

"Did we get them boss?"

"Be quiet Leopold!" Raul snapped, still waving the statue above his head. "The relics are fake you stupid animals! What are you doing?"

One or two of the rebels had begun to listen, but already it was too late. Jack and his crew were clear of the square.

Moving to the very back of the bus, to be as far away from Raul and the others, Samuel ran his fingers through Maria's tangled hair as she let her head rest in his lap. Michael and David sat nervously together a few rows down, while Jack, still pointing the shotgun at Raul through the open window, carefully studied them all.

"Is everything alright? Any cuts or bruises?"

The two Americans shook their heads.

"Let's just get out of here," Samuel eventually replied, his eyes caught between the Colombians outside and the Colombian in his care. Watching Leopold climb to his feet, Jack turned to the bus driver.

"When you're ready Miguel."

Miguel nodded and thumped his foot onto the pedal. As the bus tore away, the Colombians outside finally realized their mistake. One of Raffa's men was the first to fire. His shot missed the bus by a mile but was enough to set them all off.

As the bullets began to fly, whizzing past their ears, both Raul and Leopold, now weapon less, threw themselves into the dirt. Jack was jogging down the buses central isle, humming to himself, when, through the window, Michael spotted Joseph sprawled across the square, not far from where Raul and Leopold had thrown themselves.

"Jesus! Stop the bus, we gone and forgot Joe!"

"Screw Joe! We can't turn back now," Jack snapped, having reached Samuel. Michael was already on his feet and racing toward Miguel when Jack fired the first warning shot. Michael froze, the bullet just skimming past his head and smashing into the buses large, front window. Its glass shattered, missing Miguel only by luck and inches.

"Not one more step Michael, there's a good lad."

"We ain't leaving Joe behind!" the American screamed, spinning around.

"You gotta go back Jack...He's just a kid," David added.

"Nobody is going back! Now be seated!"

"We can't just leave him dad, for Christ's sake, they'll rip him apart." The gunshot had jolted Maria awake and now she sat upright; startled.

"Sam?" she began to whisper.

"It's okay Maria, I'm still here."

"Why all the shouting? I thought we got away now?"

Samuel eyed his father angrily.

"In all the excitement we went and forgot somebody."

"Who? Who we forget?"

"Joseph, we left Joseph behind."

"Then we must go back for him!"

"I'm afraid it's too late now Maria. It's far too dangerous," Jack tried to explain, half his attention still fixed on Michael.

"But he is just a boy!"

"I know damn well what he is Maria, so don't start on at me!"

"Hey, don't you go speaking to her like that," Samuel warned.

"Looks like everyone's against you Jack," David interrupted.

"Should listen to what people say!"

It was at that precise moment that Jack noticed the absence of one other very important object.

"By the way Samuel, who has the suitcase?"

Samuel paused.

"Joseph, Joseph had the case last."

"Miguel! Turn this bleeding bus around!" Jack bellowed, sprinting back down the central isle, brushing Michael easily to one side as he barged past. The bus was screeching to a halt as Jack reached the driver. "Well? What are you waiting for? Spin her around! We have a boy to rescue!"

"I no go back Senor," Miguel whimpered, his hands clutching the steering wheel for dear life.

Within the bat of an eyelid, Jack had grabbed hold of the Colombian's shirt collar and thrown him to the deck.

"Seen more life in a bleeding morgue," he mumbled, grasping the steering wheel himself.

"Hey, Raul, you see what I see?" Leopold whispered, looking past the heaps of bodies which now lay heaped before him, having noticed the bus turning around. As expected, nearly all of Raffa's men had been wiped out by this point, Raffa and Saul included. Now heavily outnumbered by the remaining rebels, those that had survived their onslaught, surrendered.

"Raul, I see the bus, it's comin' back!" Slowly, Raul lifted his head from the dirt. To his surprise, Leopold was correct. Indeed the bus was speeding back across the square toward them.

"They must be crazy!" Leopold continued.

"Just greedy my little American friend, just greedy."

A few of the rebels were already turning to look at the bus. Knowing he had to act fast, Raul shouted over to them:

"Hey, boys, they comin' back for your gold! You gonna let them?" In unison, the remaining rebels spun around.

~ ~ ~

"Get your head lower Samuel," Jack advised. "And remember; don't start shooting until I give the order!"

Samuel, crouching down beside his father, peered nervously through the buses shattered windscreen. They were only yards away from the rebels who were already training their automatic weapons on the approaching bus. Shaking badly, Samuel held his pistol in both hands. He wasn't sure who to shoot first until he spotted Raul and Leopold fronting the rebel group, and from that point on he knew exactly who to aim at.

Maria, having refused to let Samuel face the danger alone, now clung to his waist with Michael and David huddled together beside the buses doors. Jack pressed down harder on the accelerator.

"I'm going to run the bus right through the buggers so listen up! We'll not have time to stop...Going to separate Joe from the rest of the group...When the doors open be ready to grab him...Got that Michael?"

"Just get me in place Jack."

"Good stuff...You alright down there Samuel?"

"As I'll ever be!"

"Then hold tight son, and start bloody shooting!"

Even as he spoke, the rebels, headed by Raul, opened fire. Automatically, Samuel threw himself under the dashboard as the bullets began to ping off the bus, and it took him several seconds before he was able to lift his head.

"Now, Samuel! Now!" Jack screamed, his own head buried beneath the steering wheel, only just able to see where he was going. Using all the courage he could muster, Samuel took aim and fired off his first volley.

As Jack had hoped, the rebels, seeing that the bus was not about to stop any time soon, began a panicked sprint to their right in a bid to escape the oncoming monster; leaving Joseph, still sprawled out across the ground, on Michael's left hand side. Reaching the boy's exact spot, Jack slammed on the brakes. The doors flew open and Michael, not waiting for the bus to stop, launched himself outside. By this point all but one of the buses windows had been shot through.

Although heavily outgunned, Samuel continued to take the odd shot through one of the window openings. The handful of rebel soldiers, who now remained, zigzagged this way and that across the square, letting rip with their automatic rifles every so often. They had no solid cover in which to hide themselves and so a few of the more agile combatants had taken to rolling about the ground in their attempts to avoid Samuel's careful aim. With one or two men by his side, it might very well have turned into a turkey shoot, but neither Michael nor David had been entrusted with a gun.

"What the hell were you playing at kid?" Michael scolded, having just managed to drag a terrified Joseph onto the bus. The kid didn't reply, his face a sickly white, his hands still clinging to the case.

"You could have got us all killed!"

"Is he hurt?" Jack asked above the crackling gunfire, already pushing the bus back up to full speed.

"Yeah, I think he's okay, just scared shitless I guess."

Samuel was down to his last bullet as Jack began to spin the bus back around. Seeing this and sensing that their loot was at last safe, the majority of the rebels gave up shooting. Only

Raul, Leopold and two other soldiers continued their violent assault as the bus turned tail.

"Kill them," Maria calmly instructed.

Through the shattered window she watched them, Raul in particular, a satisfied smile covering her tired face.

"Kill them Samuel," she repeated, this time louder. But Samuel was already stuffing the pistol back into his belt.

"What are you doing?"

"It's all over Maria, we got away."

Her smile vanished.

"I said kill them you fool!"

She tried to grab the pistol for herself but Samuel was too quick. He'd just about managed to get her hands under control when another burst of automatic fire ripped through the bus, one of the bullets splitting Samuel's right ear in half.

"Jesus!"

"Samuel!"

With thick blood now pouring down his neck, Samuel whipped the pistol free from his belt and again took aim. Raul and the others were now mere dots in the distance. He tried to blank the stinging pain from the bullet wound but found the task impossible. Running short on time, he quickly selected his target and fired. As he fired, a final volley of bullets filled the bus.

"Keep your heads down!" Jack yelled, one of the bullets having whizzed past his own ear.

"We're not safe and dry yet people, so stay on your toes!"

Nobody on the bus needed to be told twice. With the pistol now empty, all six escapees had thrown themselves to the deck, ignoring the broken glass which covered the buses floor. They all suffered minor cuts in the process but none of them complained, knowing how close death had come.

Still keeping his head down, Jack finally steered the bus clear of the square.

~ ~ ~

"Keep firing guys!" With the threat of retaliation now gone, Leopold had suddenly found the courage to fire his gun at the fleeing bus. However, no longer feeling repressed, he'd gone overboard, outrunning Raul and the two soldiers in his childlike desire to shed blood. Even a lack of bullets did nothing to dent this insane hunger, and only when his lungs had begun to feel like bursting, did he stop running. Both hands now resting on his knees, he glanced back across the square to find his companions. But something was wrong, dreadfully wrong.

The rebel soldiers had stopped their running too. Side by side, they now hovered over Raul's lifeless body. Leopold was very nearly sick as he caught up with the pair, having to look away the second he saw for himself what had happened to his boss.

"Jesus Christ almighty!"

The words hardly did the scene justice. Now laying stone dead with his mouth open and his eyes startled wide, Raul Morales stared back up at the three men. Apart from his look of shock, Samuel's final bullet had not left a single mark across the Colombian's large, chubby face. Instead, the top half of Raul's head had been blown apart by the bullet's impact, the colourful contents of his shattered skull now scattered all over the surrounding square. As Leopold and the others continued to study their grisly find, a dozen or so hungry birds, each one of them eager for a piece of tiny brain or loose flap of skin, began to swoop down and fight one another for the privilege of feasting first.

"I guess that's one less we'll have to share gold with, hey guys?" Leopold tried to joke. The humour fell flat and a second later, just as one of the birds made off with an especially large chunk of prime Colombian brain, he was sick down the front of his shirt. Seeing this, the two soldiers who were with him chuckled.

Jack didn't wait for the kids outside to disperse. Just as soon as the bus had come to a standstill he was reaching for the suitcase, only recently untangled from Joseph's fingers.

"Why we stopping Jack? Hell, we ain't even outa town yet!" Michael asked, still laid flat across the floor. The street kids, curious with their new arrival, had already begun to claw their way through the shattered windows. Covered in broken glass and other bits of bus, Michael brushed himself down and crawled over to where Jack was opening the case. Miguel, still hiding behind one of the seats, decided to stay put, convinced that Jack had not paid him enough for what he'd been put through.

"It's all still here thank God," Jack spoke, quickly flicking through the numerous bundles of cash. However, Joseph didn't share his enthusiasm:

"But was it really worth it?"

"Oh, I should have thought so young man."

"Don't suppose we get to share a little of your good fortune too?" David added. Jack chuckled.

"I'm afraid not."

To reinforce his point, Jack picked up Samuel's pistol which lay hidden beneath one of the seats and pointed it at all three Americans.

"So don't go getting any ideas...Okay?"

"Killjoy," Michael complained.

"Samuel, you can get up now."

Jack had turned to find his son still slumped over Maria.

"Samuel? Did you hear what I said? It's safe to get up now."

Still no reply. Dropping the last bundle back into the case, Jack walked over to where his son lay and began to shake him.

"Samuel? Samuel lad, wake up."

Gripping his son's shoulder, he rolled him over. Mildly concerned, Michael and the others had sauntered over also.

"Samuel. You can..."

Jack's hand froze, his fingers, long and now trembling, hovering just above his son's head.

"Samuel?"

Samuel was dead; shot in the back, a gaping wound revealed as Jack had turned him over. The seat was now soaked in blood also. It dripped slowly onto the floor where a tiny, scarlet pool had quickly formed. Gently, Michael placed a hand across Jack's shoulder.

"Hey, I think you should sit down for a while."

"What?"

"I said I think you should take a seat Jack."

Maria was dead too. Having passed through Samuel, the guilty bullet had lodged itself firmly into her lower spine. Jack was about to kneel next to his son when, turning quickly, he brushed away Michael's hand.

"Jack?"

"Well, I suppose we'll leave them both to rest then, can't blame the buggers, been a stressful day, make them something nice to eat once we're all safe."

"Jack, just wait a second fella."

But Jack was already behind the wheel of the bus, twisting its ignition key. He made several attempts to bring the monster back to life, but she refused point blank.

"I'll wake them up once we're clear of town, the sleep should do them good."

Michael and the others, seizing the opportunity, were now leaving the bus, Michael having grabbed the suitcase for himself. He'd reached the road outside when Jack, still trying to get the bus moving again, caught a glimpse of him.

"Michael? Boys? Are you leaving us already?"

For a moment all three Americans froze.

"It's time to go Jack. You take real good care now," Michael replied softly.

Jack had left his pistol beside Samuel. The American, never one to miss a trick, had quickly taken it for himself. At that very moment his hand hovered over its shiny, steel barrel. Despite his terrible shock, Jack was quick to notice this, and notice too the battered suitcase that was no longer his.

"You hear what I say Jack?"

Very slowly, with a look of complete despair, Jack nodded.

"Yes Michael, I hear what you say."

Reaching into the half opened suitcase the American then, unexpectedly, threw Jack a small bundle of cash. Somewhat surprised by the gesture, Jack caught the bundle first time, all but a few of its notes now smeared in a thick, drying blood.

"I hope you don't expect a thank you."

"Just take care of yourself Jack and hey, maybe now you'll think about going straight."

"Well, I can always think about it."

With a brief wave of his hand, Michael left to join his companions. For almost a minute, Jack sat in silence, watching the Americans disappear in the rear view mirror. Dropping the bundle of cash into his shirt pocket, he again tried to start the bus. This time, after only one attempt, she began to purr. His hands were already shifting gear when he remembered the street kids, and turned to find one of the bleeders rummaging through Samuel's trousers.

"Get away from him!"

The boy paused, smiled along with his other friends, and began the search all over. He only backed away when he saw Jack charging down the aisle toward him and only then because the smaller children had taken fright first and scuttled off toward the far end of the bus.

"Go on...Beat it!"

The skinny kid waved a crumpled fifty dollar note in Jack's face and made his escape through the back window. With the beast's engine still ticking over, although very nearly on the brink of collapse, Jack sank down next to his son.

"I'm sorry Samuel. Truly I am."

Outside, he could hear the children laughing as they celebrated their financial gain. He thought he heard the Americans too, but the distant voices soon revealed their Colombian accents. He glanced back down toward Samuel. Something had caught his eye. A small leather pouch, no bigger than a packet of crisps with the initials JL embroiled in faded white across its skin, could be seen poking out from inside Samuel's jacket pocket.

"Oh, Sammy. You poor boy."

Gently, Jack lifted the pouch from its hiding place and slowly began to empty its glittering contents across the buses blooded floor. Wiping a tear from his eye, he whispered:

"Gypsy gold Sammy. Gypsy gold."

The gold doubloons, twelve in total, now slowly began to vanish as they each settled into Samuel's thick blood. As they completely disappeared from sight, Miguel appeared.

"I suppose you'll want dropping off some place?" Jack spoke quietly. Still more than a little dazed, Miguel was unable to offer a reply. Not waiting for a response, Jack stood and returned to the driver's seat. His fingers were already toying with the ignition key when he felt Miguel's hand over his.

"You must leave them here Senor."

"When I want your advice Miguel, I'll ask for it."

"The police at border control will have questions too Jack...Real difficult questions."

Jack let his hand slip from the ignition.

"I'll not leave my son here Miguel, not in Sevilla."

"I don't think we have much choice, time is not on our side!"

"Always options old son, always options, and please, will you quit with all this 'we' business. This is my problem, mine to sort out alone."

Miguel was looking past Jack as he lectured; into the deserted street beyond. Something had caught the Colombian's eye. It was a sight which twisted his stomach inside out. Where their road wound itself out of view, dividing off into other alleys and thoroughfares, the distant, flashing lights of approaching vehicles were now visible.

"If you tell me where you live I'll gladly drop you off old boy...Then I must be on my way Miguel," Jack continued, completely oblivious to the new danger. Taking Jack's chattering head firmly in his hands, Miguel levered it toward the oncoming convoy.

"Bugger," Jack mumbled.

"Government troops Senor, I think we get going now, Si?"

Not wasting a second, Jack quickly stung the bus back into life. As he did, Miguel counted five jeeps in all, each of them packed to capacity with government soldiers. Their dust covered registration plates were very nearly visible as Jack steered the bus clear of the main road and into one of the smaller streets.

"You think they saw us?"

"I think we got away with it," Jack answered, his eyes on the rear view mirror. A few very long seconds later and the convoy sped past, throwing up huge balls of dust as they went.

"Jesus, that was close."

"So, where do we go now Miguel? I'm buggered if I know where to go."

"Just keep following the road ahead Senor, you can hide out at my place for the time being."

"Very thoughtful."

Miguel lived ten miles outside Sevilla. He lived on a small farm along with his young wife, Consuela, and their two kids. During the entire journey, Jack had not spoken a single word. He kept his eyes permanently fixed on the road ahead, listening to Miguel's erratic directions. Miguel had found this all very disconcerting and was glad when at last they reached his farm.

Parking the bus behind the estate's one barn, Miguel had then ushered Jack quickly inside the farmhouse proper, Jack doing his very best to avoid the jumble of chickens which scratched and pecked their way happily about the main yard.

Consuela, slim with long, dark hair, threw her arms around her husband just as soon as he'd stepped through the door; their two children, both boys no older than four, tugging frantically at their father's worn trouser legs in a bid for recognition. Watching all this, Jack was made to feel increasingly uneasy. Usually the life and soul of any party, he stood looking awkward a few sheepish paces behind Miguel, trying to muster enough energy for even a simple hello.

As it was, when the time came, Consuela all but ignored him, already knowing the dangerous nature of her husband's work and guessing that Jack was somehow behind it all. He had to make do with a brief handshake, which was fine. Far from feeling put out, Jack had welcomed the cool reception, reassuring Miguel later on that evening that no explanations were required for his wife's cool behavior.

The family gathered for their main supper at around eight. Reluctantly, Jack agreed to join them. As expected, the conversation was strained from the very beginning and continued thereafter. The two boys, not used to such solemn occasions and secretly fascinated by their strange visitor, sat quietly between Jack and their father, only speaking when spoken to, in much the same manner as Jack.

A short time after supper, Jack asked to be shown to his room. Unnerved by the peculiar atmosphere which had fallen into his home, Miguel was more than happy to oblige. Reaching the stairs, he explained to Jack that he could stay for one night only and that he should be gone by first light. Jack could only find the strength to nod a reply and made for his bed.

He slept well, despite the day's tragic events, and come six the following day he was already awake and eager to be gone. Miguel had not bothered to see him off but, to his surprise, he found Consuela waiting for him downstairs. She placed a large bag into his hands and kissed him once on either cheek. He took a glimpse inside the bag and found three oranges, one banana and several slices of bread. Knowing this was more than they could afford, Jack placed a hundred dollar bill beneath a rock beside their barn before climbing aboard the bus.

Sometime during the night either Consuela or Miguel, Jack was pretty sure it had been Consuela, had draped a large blanket across the two bodies, a gesture that Jack was very grateful for.

"Time to go home you old dog," he muttered to himself, sticking the bus into gear. Driving away from the farm, he caught sight of Consuela standing in her doorway. He couldn't be sure, but he thought she was crying.

~ ~ ~

After the fire fight had come to an end, it had taken the terrified inhabitants of Sevilla a further four hours before the bravest amongst them had even dared to look out their windows. Noting the dead bodies which had been left to decay across the main square, it wasn't long before, one by one, the locals then left the safety of their homes and wandered, bewildered looking, outside. By this time, rigor mortis had long set in and it had taken a myriad of hammers and saws in order to prize the statuettes free from each dead man's grip.

The Thief's Son

With no police; and no mayor to organize such a force, it was left to Sevilla's inhabitants to clear away the mess. A huge bonfire was lit at the very heart of the square, the largest bonfire in Sevilla's long and blooded history. Later that evening, in honour of their new found wealth, a huge party was held. It went on for almost two days running, the longest celebration that anyone could recall.

Two miles south of Santa Marta, Jack Locke splashed the buses battered interior with what little petrol remained in his can. Bidding a final goodbye to Samuel and Maria, he then set it alight. He sat down beside the road's wide, grass verge and watched the coach as it slowly disintegrated. He'd picked a quiet back road for the ceremony. No cars or trucks came even remotely close as the bus burned. As night fell only a solitary Colombian appeared on horseback along the isolated dirt track.

Drawing close and spotting Jack, lying flat on his back; his eyes toward the heavens, the curious horseman stopped to ask what had happened. Jack was more than glad to unload his unhappy tale, but when it was told and the Colombian laughed, not having believed a single word of it, Jack simply shrugged and laid back down to rest.

The bus continued to burn well into the next morning. By early afternoon, cool enough to approach at last, Jack left his grass side vigil and strolled mournfully over to what was left of the coach. Scraping up what ashes he could into what should have been his water bottle, he then set off once again along the dirt track. Santa Marta was not far off. From there, he would return to England. He didn't have a clue what to do with Samuel's ashes.

Printed in Great Britain
by Amazon